ON WINGS OF DEATH—

Heat seared the back of Larson's neck, and he ran, even as he thought, *Dragon. Goddamned fire-breathing dragon like every legend and fairy tale I've ever read.*

A wall of trees rose before him. With a joyous sob, Larson ran between them. Yet even here there was scant safety as flame gouted through the trees with a heat that made him scream. Clutching his sword, Larson ran on with a speed born of desperation. Branches rustled overhead, too loud for wind. Fire lanced before Larson, the stabbing fires coming closer and closer, threatening to set the entire forest ablaze. Spotting the light of a campfire in the distance, Larson fled toward this one possible chance of aid. Flame shot down, and a wall of heat knocked Larson to one knee at the edge of the camp. "Dragon!" he screamed his warning through lungs that felt raw. "Fire ... breathing ... dragon!"

MICKEY ZUCKER REICHERT

GODSLAYER

DAW BOOKS, INC.
DONALD A. WOLLHEIM, PUBLISHER

1633 Broadway, New York, NY 10019

DAW Book Collectors No. 716.

Acknowledgments
The Spaewife's Song; as quoted in *Gods of the North* by Brian
Branston, published by Thames and Hudson; copyright © 1955 and
1980 by Brian Branston.

Conrad, Joseph, lines from *Under Western Eyes*; copyright © 1911;
reprinted by permission of the trustees for the Joseph Conrad estate,
and by permission of Doubleday & Company, Inc.

First Printing, August, 1987

1 2 3 4 5 6 7 8 9

PRINTED IN THE U.S.A.

*For the veterans of Vietnam, especially
the PTSD patients of Coatesville VA Hospital.
May they find an uncondemning world and
a god who believes in them.*

And for

*Marcellus, Brahmin, and Ahngmar for the
inspiration.*

ACKNOWLEDGMENTS

I would like to thank Janny Wurts for being a role model, a teacher, and a friend; Joel Rosenberg for slapping me around when I most needed it; Raymond Feist for glowing praise and encouragement; Steve Zucker for storybook heroics; Jane Butler for her godawful patience and "not to worry"; Sheila Gilbert for things that can't be said in public; John Mulvey for objectivity, encouragement, and enthusiasm; my mother for patience; my father for pretending to discourage me; but mostly Mark Fabi for not writing a satire.

CONTENTS

PROLOGUE

---

*"I! I who fashioned myself a sorcerer or
an angel, Who dispensed with all moral-
ity, I have come back to the earth."*
—Arthur Rimbaud, Adieu

The three mailed guards who ushered Bramin into
the king's court regarded him with cautious curiosity. No one dared touch him. Nor did they question the cloth parcel which swung from his belt.
Offending any wizard could spell instant death,
and the jade stone clamped in the black-nailed
claw which tipped Bramin's staff identified him as
a sorcerer of high rank.

As they passed through the double set of oak
doors, Bramin fought to keep his head high. The
battle he had just survived and the enchantments
of transport weakened him both mentally and
physically. His aura had dulled to a flicker of gold
and, though he had nothing to fear in Ashemir's
throne room, he hoped the king's magician would
not recognize his fatigue. It was simply a matter of
pride.

The carpeted path to the king's throne seemed

11

to stretch for miles. The court watched the procession in a vast silence which jagged Bramin's already taut nerves. A comma of black hair slipped into his eye, and he flicked it back with an anger that sapped much of his remaining strength. Weakness of any sort enraged Bramin, and it reminded him of his reckless squandering of power. Overconfidence had cost many of his colleagues their lives.

"Step forward and name yourself." King Ashemir's command broke the silence, and tense whispers followed it. Ire rose momentarily at this ritual formality. The king knew Bramin well. The magician had been born and raised in the royal city, the product of a rape. His father was one of the dark elves, the last faery creature seen in this part of the world. As a child, Bramin paid for his willowy figure and dark complexion with jeerings and ridicule.

Bramin came forward, unhurried. He nodded briefly at the advisor beside the king, glared at the court sorcerer, who regarded him with both envy and amusement, and bowed pleasantly to the king. "I am Bramin, Dragonrank of the Jade Claw." He thumped the base of his staff on the floor for emphasis. "I have performed your quest. The giant, Redselr, lies dead at my hands." He thumbed the sack at his belt. Enervation and anxiety caused him to misjudge position and strength, and the tie snapped. The bag fell to the floor, and the giant's head rolled free to the king's feet.

King Ashemir recoiled with a gasp. The court sorcerer turned an unbecoming shade of green. Behind Bramin, strained whispers broke to cries of fear and amazement. Guards scrambled to maintain order, others ran for the abomination which seemed to stare at their king with glazed eyes.

With a word and a gesture, Bramin caused the head to slide back into its bag. The effort slammed against him like a wall, stealing his breath. His life aura flickered dangerously. A high-pitched ringing filled his head, making the voices around him seem distant. Yet Bramin retained control over his languishing muscles. Gradually his mind cleared, and he cursed himself brutally. He could have let the guards clear his mistake away or physically done so himself. Pride alone goaded him to recklessness, and he had nearly paid its price.

The king cleared his throat. His look of fear dissolved, masked by a pleasant smile. "You've earned your reward, Bramin Halfman. Five chests of gold, a parcel of land, or the hand of my daughter, Halfrija. The choice is yours."

The pronouncement of Halfrija's name made Bramin smile despite his exhaustion and indignation. "I need neither money nor power, for I have both already. But for Halfrija's hand, I would stop the sun from setting and the moon from rising. I would still the tides or steal the hammer of Thor."

The court passed opinion in a gentle hum of conversation. The king bit his lip against an ecstatic grin, but his blue eyes gleamed with excitement as they met Bramin's glowing red glare. The court sorcerer looked stricken. All three men knew Bramin would need to abandon the School of Dragonrank, since one of its primary requirements was eleven months per year of training on the school's grounds. For the king, it meant a new court magician with power beyond any of his predecessors. Only those blessed with the claw symbol could join the Dragonranks. Its devotees were the most capable users of the art, and the most able among them became omnipotent lords or directly served gods. "Summon Halfrija," Ashemir commanded his guards. They rushed to obey.

Bramin knew marriage would force him to sacrifice a future of ultimate power for domesticity and the banality of court proceedings. He lowered his head, staring at the claw-shaped scar which puckered the black skin on the back of his right hand. The symbol had appeared at the age of ten along with the first traces of the life aura which glimmered about him, visible only to those versed in magic. His mother and human half siblings sent Bramin away that year. So he traded the gibes of the citizens of Forste-Mar for their respect and the grueling discipline of the Dragonrank.

A person marked with the claw was a rare enough occurrence in any town, and Forste-Mar received its second surprise three years later. Bramin's eldest half sister, Silme, was similarly stamped by destiny. She joined the Dragonrank, which pleased Bramin. It gave him a familiar companion on his infrequent breaks from studying enchantments or practicing swordsmanship. And he had always liked Silme best. Many times she had dried his tears or soothed his deadly rages when children grew cruel with their taunts or citizens wounded his pride with derision.

The doors swung open, interrupting his memories, and the court again fell silent as the guards ushered Halfrija before them. A dress of blue silk with interlacing patterns of silver tastefully outlined her delicate frame. Her face was fair with artistically high cheek bones. Her wide-set eyes were the pale blue of cornflowers. At the sight of the lady he loved, all other thought fled Bramin.

His heart pounded, pumping warmth and desire through his body. He stared without speaking, love-blinded to her taut-lipped pall of fear.

The king rose from his throne. "Bramin Jade-claw, you see my daughter, the Lady Halfrija. On Midsummer's Day, I sanction the marriage between you. May you live long together and prosper!"

Halfrija opened her mouth to speak, but her words were lost beneath the cheers of the crowd. As Bramin turned his back to the king and trod the walkway toward Halfrija, she shrank back. Her hands clenched to bloodless fists, and her soprano pierced the dying shouts of the court. "Wait!"

Bramin stopped before her trembling form.

"I would test your love," she announced shrilly. "It is my right."

Breath broke from Bramin in an angry hiss. He had risked his life for her once and would gladly do so again. But her entreaty was an affront. While it was indeed her privilege, no princess had invoked the law since its enactment three centuries past.

Halfrija continued. "You must fight a champion of my choosing to the death in the arena at midmorn. Should you survive, my hand is yours." She shivered, and her voice acquired a strange, droning quality. "You may select your weapon, but use of sorceries or enchanted swords will free me from my promise."

Struck to the heart by the maliciousness of her challenge, Bramin dropped all pretense of dignity. He knelt before Halfrija with the true respect he had denied the king. "As you wish, my lady. May the court hear my vow to kill or be killed by your champion without use of magic."

Halfrija's mouth twitched to a cruel smile which swiftly disappeared.

Stiffly, Bramin turned. Fatigue and hopelessness wove a black curtain across his vision. As he retreated along the carpeted walkway he stumbled, and the glares of courtiers sapped him of all remaining grace. It seemed an eternity before he reached the far end of the hall. A guard swung open the carved oak doors, and Bramin passed through them. The portals clanged closed behind him, silencing the whispered condemnations of Ashemir's court as completely as death.

Outside, wind flung strands of matted hair into Bramin's face as if to mock him. Despair rose to self-pity, then flared to righteous anger. His journey through the familiar streets of his childhood seemed as one through a tunnel. The dirt roads blurred to the dark obscurity of disinterest. Peasants stared or scuttled from his path, unnoticed. A horse cart driver hurled epithets at the dark sorcerer who paced the cobbles at the center of the alley. But at a flick of Bramin's hand, the driver stemmed his tide of oaths and swerved to a roadside ditch. *They fear me.* For the first time since he had left to kill the giant, Bramin smiled with cruel satisfaction. *My life aura has dwindled to nearly nothing, yet those who once scorned me now shy from a gesture.* Still, for Halfrija's love, he would weather the gibes of peasants gladly.

The setting sun lanced red light through the guttering remnant of Bramin's aura. Utterly alone in his fury despite the dispersing throng of Forste-Mar's citizenry, he plodded to his mother's home. He opened the simple plank door, stepped across its threshold, and slammed it closed behind him. Despite his effort, the portal slid shut with an

impotent click which betrayed his weakness. Rage
flared anew.

Despite the death of Bramin's stepfather several
months earlier, the cottage had changed little since
his childhood. The sod-chinked walls enclosed a
simply-furnished room separated from his mother's bedchamber by a patched, blue curtain. Silme
sat before a blazing hearth fire, a tomcat nestled
in the folds of her robe, while a brother and sister
begged stories of distant lands and Dragonrank
training. As Bramin entered, his mother rose from
a chipped wooden bench, her youngest child cradled to her breast. "Bramin?"

Bramin gave no explanation. He spared neither
glance nor words for the mother and half siblings
who followed his march to the loft ladder with
questioning stares. Anger lent the sorcerer strength.
He caught the lowest rungs in callused palms and
climbed to his sleeping quarters with a deliberate-
ness designed to override fatigue-inspired clumsi-
ness. Once in the loft, he pitched onto a pallet,
oblivious to the bells and balls left by the child
who occupied this bed since Bramin's departure
to pursue the skills of Dragonrank. Tears burned
his eyes. Repeatedly, his fist pounded the pillow,
scattering straw among the toys.

Behind Bramin, the ladder groaned. Silme's sweet
voice wound through the loft. "Brother, are you
well?"

Bramin whirled like a cornered beast. Inappropriately, his malice channeled against the half
sister who had comforted him in youth, the one
woman he knew would not condemn him. "Nothing's changed, Silme! The citizens of Forste-Mar
still hate me. Halfrija spurns my love." He struck
the pallet again.

"Stop!" Silme's voice grew uncharacteristically harsh. "Before you embed your soul in self-pity and accuse me of lying, tell me what happened in Ashemir's court."

Bramin sucked air through pursed lips, then exhaled in a long sigh. He recounted the scenario in the king's presence, his overwhelming exhaustion, Ashemir's eager determination, and Halfrija's cruelty. As he concluded the tale, he surrendered to the cold grip of hopelessness. His words emerged in a thin whine. "While vestiges of dignity remain, I must leave Forste-Mar and never return. I cannot bear the sight of Halfrija's beauty, knowing her love will never belong to me."

Silme lowered herself to the pallet beside her half brother. She squeezed his knee reassuringly. "Don't talk that way, Bramin. Your loves are intense. Your hatreds fester. In youth, you would damn all children for a single taunt and despise every man of Forste-Mar for a glare. Now, Bramin, would you condemn yourself to exile to avoid a challenge?"

"A challenge!" Bramin shook free from Silme's grip. "Halfrija degraded me by calling upon a privilege rejected for centuries. Even Queen Agnete, who wrote the law, never invoked it for herself or her daughters."

Silme's reply came soft as a cat's purr. "But Halfrija knew you could fulfill it."

"What?"

Silme framed a smile of triumph. "Halfrija doesn't hate you. For the last decade you have trained in a distant land eleven months of the year. Yet Halfrija never married in your absence."

Bramin scowled, unconvinced.

Silme rose from the pallet and knelt before

Bramin. She caught his hands. "Here a woman is judged by the worth of her man. She must make certain her husband can protect her from bandits and raiders."

Silme's blue-tinged aura dwarfed Bramin's, so dimmed was it with exhaustion. The jade rank sorcerer grunted. "You know I can."

Silme concurred. "I know. But magic seems more alien to Halfrija than the sharp, dark features and red-hued eyes she has learned to accept. She understands swordplay."

Bramin wavered.

Silme pressed. "Who is the best warrior in this town?"

"Me?"

Silme stood. "We both know none of Ashemir's knights can defeat you. Halfrija knows it, too."

As anger dispersed, fatigue crowded Bramin. Though Silme's explanation seemed implausible, his desire for the princess allowed him to believe. "Then why. . . ?"

Silme interrupted. "Because she's insecure. She needs to justify your appearance by displaying your talents in public. Do you find Halfrija's hand more valuable than the life of a soldier?"

Realization drove Bramin's voice to a whisper. "Far more." He sprawled across the pallet, drained of all emotion except the early, fine stirrings of hope. As Silme crept back to the ladder, sleep overtook him. Yet, despite his half sister's reassurances, the memory of Halfrija's fleeting sneer haunted Bramin's dreams.

Rest restored the vitality drained by Bramin's battle with the giant. As he dressed in a simple tunic and breeks, many thoughts plagued him. As

skilled with a sword as with magic, Bramin knew
from his one month a year at home that no warrior of Forste-Mar could best him. Unless some
strange and highly capable swordsman had joined
them in the past year, he could not be defeated.

Bramin fastened his sword belt and drew the
blade from its leather hip scabbard. He smiled as
the radiance of his restored life aura bounced
blue highlights from the steel. He felt strong, mentally and physically. Striding from his mother's
cottage, he let the door swing shut behind him
and trotted through the streets to the cleared patch
of castle grounds. Guards passed cautiously about
him, attentive to their duties. With magically enhanced hearing, Bramin invaded their conversations, but the sentries seemed as curious about the
princess' champion as he himself.

Bramin executed an elegant series of sword
feints. The hilt felt comfortable in his grip, metal
wrapped with rough leather which would not slip
from his sweat-slicked palm. He stopped, not wishing to tire himself before the match. His love for
Princess Halfrija had begun as a childhood crush.
He sent flowers and trinkets. Though she acknowl-
edged none of them and regarded him with the
same scorn as the other citizens of Forste-Mar, her
reluctance only strengthened his passion. During
his vacations from the School of Dragonrank, he
wooed her. Soon, his love became an all-encompassing desire.

The sun shouldered over the horizon. Citizens
drifted toward the southern side of the castle
grounds where the arena towered over the quarters of guards and servants. Finely-dressed courtiers strode in regal pairs. Peasants in worn homespun crowded toward the building, hoping to catch

a glimpse of the combatants. Armored guards tried to maintain some order in the milling chaos with little success.

From habit, Bramin checked his own excitement. As he walked toward the arena, he took his staff in hand. It would help him through the throng, for men rightly shied from its touch. He used it like a walking stick, though none would question his youth or vigor; even those too foolish to fear the power of his magic could not fail to notice the unearthly aura of evil inherited from his father.

The citizens of Forste-Mar shrank from the slim, dark wizard who strode purposefully to the door of the stadium. Despite the demoralizing inevitability of combat, Bramin gleaned some amusement from their awe. Years ago, these same men and women would have spit on him.

The guards gestured Bramin inside, and the crowd closed in behind him, hoping for a glimpse of the combat. Noblemen lined the balconies and applauded politely at his entrance. Bramin leaned his staff against the lowest stands, walked to center ring, and examined his audience. He raised a hand in greeting to the king and queen. Ashemir waved, then shrugged in apology. Halfrija's seat was unoccupied, and Bramin supposed she was coaching her champion. The thought formed a painful ball in his throat. He felt utterly alone. Now, before Forste-Mar's masses, Silme's reassurances rang as hollow as in youth when she swore her playmates did not hate him even as they hurled rocks and challenges. Anxiety allowed Bramin to forget the times she had stroked his hair until he ceased to tremble. He knew nothing of how she had confronted his tormentors with their inhumanity and made them blush with humility.

Thus reminded of the townspeople's hostility, Bramin's will faltered. The noise of the peasants changed pitch. The door swung open, and Halfrija entered. She wore a suit of leather far too large for her tiny frame. She grasped a long sword in both fists, and it leaned awkwardly.

The audience erupted in riot. The queen fainted. All color drained from the king, and he sat, rigid, like an ivory statue. Bramin met Halfrija halfway into the ring. "What are you doing?" he demanded.

Her eyes blazed with madness. "I *am* my champion. Kill or be killed," she chanted like a priest before a sacrifice. She thrust the sword clumsily.

Bramin's mouth went painfully dry. He side-stepped and caught both of Halfrija's wrists, drawing her too close for combat. If anyone in the audience spoke or moved, Bramin did not notice. His blood-colored eyes probed the princess for answers, but true to his word he avoided magic. "Halfrija . . ."

She spat in his face. "Beast! I would rather die than marry you."

Halfrija's words pained like blows. Bramin's grip tightened on her flesh till she winced. His voice was rambling and plaintive as a lost child. "Why? Oh, why, Halfrija? I've the power to grant your every desire. A thousand kings have offered great treasures for me to come serve them. Yet I refused them all for you. I love you, Halfrija."

Halfrija's hands whitened as her face flushed with ugly rage. "I'll not be disdained by my own people because a dark creature loves me." She added cruelly, "If, indeed, your kind can know love."

Bramin caught his breath with a sob. "Now I know love and pain." Desperately, he spouted Silme's trite comforts as if they were truths. "The people of Forste-Mar don't hate me. They mis-treated me as a child from ignorance. But many years have passed since . . ."

"You stupid animal!" Halfrija's voice rose in pitch and volume. "We hate you now more than ever. We would kick and spit, even slay you if we didn't fear your power. You're no man, you're a beast. Worse than a beast, for a rat is content with its lot and you have the audacity to pretend you're human!"

Slapped by Halfrija's cruelty, Bramin made a pained noise. His grip went lax. "Halfrija . . ."

Her sword struck. Though too near her target for an effective strike, her blade nicked Bramin's side. The razor edge opened his tunic. Blood beaded his skin. Bramin watched in fascination as a single drop slid down his breeks and splashed a tiny, scarlet circle in the sand.

He looked up as Halfrija raised her sword like a club and lashed at his face. Tears stung his eyes. He stood, hopeless and uncaring, as the blade cut above his head. Just before the blow fell, self-righteous fury warmed his blood. The will to live and claim vengeance on all who had ever wronged him replaced the anguish roused by Halfrija's scorn. He sprang aside. Her sword whisked through air where he had stood and hammered the packed sand with a crash.

Off-balance, Halfrija staggered. Bramin caught her by the throat. He drew her so close their faces nearly touched. Her cheeks and eyes paled with fear, which gave Bramin a morbid satisfaction. The legacy of his dark ancestors rose hot in his veins. "Too good for me, lady?" His voice trans-formed to an ancient croak of evil. "You're not too good for death." His hands knotted convulsively, cartilage crumbled beneath his fingers, and Halfrija fell limp against him.

Blood trickled from the corner of her thin lips, staining Bramin's hand. He looked up quickly to a condemning horde. A great shout rose from the stands, and men descended upon him. "Stop!" screamed Bramin. His cry was lost in the rising din. Clutching Halfrija's body with one arm, he raised the other. Spell words rushed from his throat. His life aura flared to blinding white. Smoke broiled from his fingers and rolled like fog across the arena floor. It struck the first wave of courtiers and roared to flame.

Screams filled Bramin's ears like song. The courtiers' charge was transformed to chaotic flight. Enchantments rolled from the half-elf's tongue. Bramin's staff leapt to his hand. Its jade stone winked once, staining the roiling magics an eerie green-blue. And when the works of sorcery cleared, all that remained of Bramin and Halfrija were five drops of blood on the sands of the arena.

Stiffly, Halfrija let the last of her garments fall to the floor of Bramin's quarters at the School of Dragonrank. She stood before him, naked. He had imagined her unclothed so many times in his dreams and desires, yet now the sight only sickened him. Her slimness transformed to a cadaverous frailty. Her breasts sagged, violet with pooled blood. Her eyes were hollow and dead. All his magic could not restore life, only simulate it. This was not Halfrija, just a crude animation which would perform as Bramin wished, without will or knowledge of its lot.

Black rage engulfed Bramin. His life aura rose to off white as he channeled his energies. Magic

lanced Halfrija's body as it fell, and the pale form
crumbled to dust. Bitterness grew like a cancer.
Bramin rose and paced. With each jagged pass,
his fist crashed against the smoothed-stone walls.
"Hate me, do they?" he screamed at the ceiling.
"Hate spawns hate."

He stared at the charred pile which had once
been the person of the princess of Forste-Mar.
One kick scattered the ashes around his quarters.
"Hatespawn I am, and so will I remain. But all
mankind shall pay for their abhorrence." His
thoughts shifted slightly. For a moment he pictured his half sister Silme, as beautiful as Halfrija
and in many ways as cruel.

Bramin paced again. "It was she who told me
they meant no harm. She blinded me to their
treacheries and laughed behind my back. She
taught me the torture of love as though it were a
pleasure and held me from my vengeance. She
goaded me to destroy my love and shame myself
before Forste-Mar's peasants. It's too late to sun-
der Halfrija's soul, but not Silme's. She will die in
torment and the manworld of Midgard with her!"

Light flashed through his quarters, dimming his
life aura to dirty yellow as another's power pulsed
against him. Bramin turned with a hiss. Before
him stood a man more beautiful than the woman
he had loved. Fine gold locks fell to his shoulders.
His dark blue eyes twinkled with cruel mischief.
He wore a strangely-tailored costume interwoven
with magics which shimmered as he moved. Arms
folded across his chest, the stranger stared at
Bramin with a grin of arrogant scorn.

"Die, human!" screamed the half-man. Power
streamed from his fingers, slowed, and fizzled to
sparks a foot before the handsome stranger.

The man laughed, sweet as rain. "Very pretty, Hatespawn. But you've much to learn."

Bramin glared. "Who are you?"

The stranger yawned, and his shirt sparkled so it nearly blinded Bramin. "I am called by many names." He chuckled. "Some even I am too polite to speak. I am Loki, first father of lies, thief of Brisingamen, evil companion of Odin, slanderer and cheat of the gods, and father of the Fenris Wolf."

Bramin's scowl wilted. His throat went dry, and he swallowed several times before attempting speech. "A god? But why . . . ?"

"Did you mean your threats, Hatespawn?" Loki frowned accusingly. "Or were they the idle ramblings of self-pity? Decide quickly. I don't waste time with fools."

Anger blazed anew. Bramin's fists clenched so tightly his fingernails bit red welts in the palms. Though sorely embittered, he chose his words with care. "I never speak idly. I will cause the downfall of man."

The corners of Loki's mouth twitched upward, and his voice lilted. "And the gods as well if you serve my cause."

Bramin started. "Gods have enlisted the aid of high claw Dragonrank. But I am only jade. Why me?"

"Because, Hatespawn." Loki's inflection almost made the title sound pleasant. "You will rise quickly through the ranks. Already the master prepares your staff for garnet. And . . ." The god leaned casually against the stone wall. "You take your swordplay as seriously as your magic. I've use of that."

Bramin focused on the shimmering patterns of Loki's shirt. "It will still take time," he said sullenly.

"I've plenty of it." Loki grinned wickedly. "And so have you. It would be wise for us both to learn patience."

Bramin scowled, saying nothing.

Loki continued. "Save your vengeance. I've something for you to remember our bargain in the meantime." The god bowed his head and his golden hair fell about his cheeks like waterfalls, obscuring his face. His hands crossed before him, fingers spread. Slowly, he drew his hands apart as he uttered sharp, harsh syllables of summoning.

Loki's fingers curled. Suddenly, his wrists flicked outward. A globe of blackness winked into place before him, marred only by the silver lines of sorcery from Loki's shirt and Bramin's aura. The ball stretched to a rod-like shape and dropped in to Loki's hands. It was a sword.

Loki raised his head. "Take it."

Bramin bit his lower lip. Hesitantly, he took a step forward and met Loki's eyes. They were chill blue, with the same contempt as the men of Forste-Mar. Anger made the half-breed more confident. He strode forward and seized the sword.

Its sheath was carved ebony. Its hilt was split leather-wrapped steel studded with fire opals, and it fit Bramin's hand comfortably. With a quick pull, he freed the blade, slim and silver, polished so fine its glow mocked enchantments. Near its hilt, runes flickered, effused with red light. For a moment, their meaning was clear to him. Then they muddled to obscurity and his memory of them as well. Bramin muttered a spell in frustration, but the writings remained just beyond com-

prehension. "What does it say?" he demanded,
hating his inability.

Loki smiled. "It's the sword's name, Helblindi.
And its purpose. Your vengeance begins when the
writings become clear to you. Know only that men
will flee from your blade, and the braver the man,
the more he must fear it."

"Helblindi." Bramin raised his brows in question. "Isn't that the name of another god?"

"Very perceptive, Hellspawn. Very perceptive."
As suddenly as he had arrived, Loki was gone. All
that remained was a rumbling of laughter which
echoed between the walls.

CHAPTER 1

Dragonslayer

*"For those whom God to ruin has
  designed,
He fits for fate, and first destroys their
  mind."*
—*Dryden*, The Hind and the Panther

Death hung like an omnipresent shadow over the fire base at Aku Nanh, Vietnam. A wave of heat rustled a circle of thirty grass huts and drummed against the quonset of messhall and infirmary. It carried the reek of burning excrement but no relief from the broiling sun.

Inside a shelter of wood frame and bamboo, a corporal slammed his cards on the table, and Al Larson looked up from his book.

"Four jacks." A grin split the corporal's owlish face as he raked in a tidy sum of cash.

"Shit," said Jamie Fisher, a streetwise black from south Philadelphia. "Big Man knows rank, eh, blood?" He glanced teasingly at Tom Dragelin who had been kneeling on the floor for the last quarter hour. Larson awaited Dragelin's inevitable retort, but the boy only continued his prayer.

"Throw in a word for me." Gavin Smith gathered the cards with a gesture of annoyance. "I'm losing."

Dragelin loosed a purse-lipped grunt of disapproval. Larson swung his leg over the side of his bunk. "Won't help. You really want to win, learn to deal off the bottom of the deck like Steve." He gestured at the corporal.

The room fell silent. The corporal's dark eyes went cold as he glared at Larson.

"What you readin', Al? *How to Win Friends?*" Fisher picked his teeth with the corner of a card.

Gavin rose. He looked at the book in Larson's hand and laughed. "It's a text book. We're stuck in hell, and he's readin' a goddamn text book."

"Hey, this is major theology." Larson set the book aside. "Christianity's mixed up. It's fine for people at home, but what good does it do us? What good did it do Danny?"

"Stop!" The corporal's single word was a threat.

Larson's eyes burned as he fought tears. Though only twenty, he was the oldest of the group except for the corporal.

Dragelin turned toward the wall.

Gavin dealt the cards. "We're dodgin' bullets while Danny's in heaven havin' tea with God. Come on, let's finish the game."

"Wait. Hear me out." Larson ran a hand through the tangled growth of his blond hair. "What's the fundamental teaching of Christianity?"

Fisher lit a cigarette. "Do unto others."

"Peace, brotherhood, and the word of God," called Dragelin from the corner.

"Exactly." Larson smiled as Dragelin stepped into his well-prepared trap. "How much of that do you see here?"

Gavin picked up his cards, swore, and slapped them to the table. "I got a piece just yesterday."

"We got ourself a brotherhood right here," added Fisher.

Gavin finished. "And Tom'll pass God's word, won't you, buddy?" He laughed.

Larson spoke over the snickers. "We're worshiping a peace god during war. Doesn't work. The Vikings had some real war gods. Get a load of this." He raised the book and read aloud. " 'Stir war!' cried Odin. 'Set men at each other's throats. Whether they wish it or not, have men rip one another to pieces. And when they lay steeped in their blood, have them rise to fight again.' "

Dragelin crossed himself.

The corporal scowled, hand over his cards.

"Fuckin'-A, man," said Fisher. "You're crazy."

"What's your point?" asked Gavin, obviously unimpressed.

For effect, Larson stood to deliver his philosophy. "Odin signified wisdom in Norse mythology. He wasn't even their war god. The real war gods helped their side in battle. That's what we need. Not some pansy who lets people smack both cheeks."

The corporal gathered the cards with a frown. "Ten o'clock, time for patrol. Draw. Lowest two on point."

The five men grew grave as each slipped a card from the deck. Larson frowned at his three. The others displayed their draws. Gavin flipped his six. "Your war gods didn't help us much. You and me play target."

Larson forced humor around the lump growing in his throat. "On the contrary. What could please a war god more than placing his follower in the most dangerous position." He donned his helmet and gripped his M-16. "Sorry about what I said, Steve."

The corporal waved a hand. Everything was forgiven before a patrol.

Al Larson and Gavin Smith left the hut first and stepped into the withering heat of afternoon. A football hit the ground before them with a thud, and Larson started. Immediately, he cursed himself. Wariness was an asset on a sniper hunt, but hyperarousal could prove worse than none at all. Larson took several deep breaths, hefted the ball, and tossed it to a grinning, sandy-haired corpsman.

Gavin sidled several paces ahead while Larson watched the corpsman's retreating figure. It seemed ludicrous. Here was this troop of trained soldiers playing games like they were in some kind of sandlot, while he and his buddies prepared for fire action in the jungle. As instinct rose like ire, he could almost forget the card game in the hut. Everybody took a turn on patrol. It just felt better when it was the other guy's turn.

Larson hurried to catch Gavin, and they strode side by side to the perimeter gate. One of the sentries yawned as he tripped the latch, and the other raised his gun in mock salute. The men made no sound as they crossed three hundred yards of tank-cleared ground and entered the steamy murk of the jungle. The ghostly cry of a macaw drowned the noise of their boots in the soft, red mud. Gavin stiffened. Larson knew his companion believed macaw calls foreshadowed death. With so many of the birds in the Vietnamese jungles, it seemed unlikely. Yet death was nearly as common. Alert, Larson moved away.

Humidity converged on them with a stench of

sewage and blood. Larson crept through brush like a shadow, tensed for a sniper's volley. For half an hour he moved, muscles knotted. Biting insects and heat weakened him, but he found nothing except jungle fauna. Larson wondered whether he should feel relieved that no snipers waited or terrified of one concealed in the trees.

Suddenly, an explosion rocked the forest behind Larson. He plunged into the mud, heart racing. An ugly scream numbed his mind till it allowed no thought. But his body reacted. He wriggled forward cautiously.

"Al." Gavin's frantic whisper came from his right. Though tinged with panic, the familiar voice soothed.

"What happened?"

"Trap," said Gavin.

Larson shuddered. The dying scream of his companion would haunt him to the end of his life. He did not want to see what remained of the others, but he could not continue until he knew their fates with certainty. Reluctantly, Larson followed Gavin.

Bellies to the ground, they crawled between the trees. Gavin stopped abruptly and loosed an oath. His body spasmed regularly as he retched. Steeling himself, Larson looked beyond at the torn bodies. His mind exploded in terror. The corporal still lived. Nothing protruded below his waist, but he breathed in a regular, shallow pattern. Larson pushed past Gavin who caught his arm.

"No, Al." Gavin's face turned the color of fatigues.

"He's alive."

"Not long," Gavin said weakly. "He won't make it to camp. If we carry him, neither will we."

"Let go." Larson tried to twist free of Gavin's grip, not certain why he had to rescue the corporal. He could imagine his own body hemorrhaging on the jungle floor, living food for rats.

A macaw shrieked four consecutive notes. Gavin shivered, and Larson pulled away.

"Wait, listen." Gavin seized the back of Larson's shirt.

Above the continuous hum of insects, they heard the faint rustle of approaching men. "Stay." Larson licked dried lips and flitted between the trunks. Ahead he saw a dozen black-clothed figures moving stealthily toward them. Larson stood, paralyzed.

Gradually, he gathered his wits and headed back to where he'd left Gavin. "Charlie. Too many for us. Hide."

Gavin nodded. "This way."

Gavin slithered to the right. The thick foliage let too little sunlight through for underbrush to grow. Trapped in the open with only trees for cover, Larson saw no means of escape. But Gavin grabbed his arm and led him to a dry river bed. Larson grew giddy with hope. They might hide between the banks while the Vietnamese passed. Gavin gestured Larson to stillness and crept farther along the stream bed. Kneeling in mud, Larson watched his companion merge into the green infinity of jungle. The rustlings grew louder, and Larson heard a gruff vocal exchange.

Gavin's pained cry broke the hush. A volley of gunfire followed. Larson's heart beat at least as loud. He could only imagine what happened, perhaps a snake bite caused Gavin's indiscretion. It no longer mattered. Larson flattened against the bank, clutching his M-16 like a teddy bear.

Limbs frozen with fear, Larson forced himself

to think rationally. The enemy knew as well as he that soldiers did not travel alone by choice. They would come looking for him. Even as he watched, a man in black circled and entered the river bed north of his position. Larson lined his sights but did not fire, unwilling to reveal his own position. The moment he did, he died.

Larson knew without seeing that another man stalked him from the south. Cornered, he needed a miracle. *God help me,* he thought. Despite his situation, the irony of his prayer struck him. Not quite ready to accept death, he hugged the bank and waited.

Death prowled closer. He let understanding settle over him. He would die, but not alone. Deliberately, Larson switched the gun setting from semi to full auto. *Freyr. You're a war god. You ought to love this.* "For my buddies, Freyr!"

Larson burst from the river bed, shooting. He embraced death.

Al Larson stared at bleak stone walls. *Alive,* he thought. *Impossible. Those guns should have cut me in half.* He ran anxious hands along his body and felt nothing abnormal but the slick sweat which coated his palms. He sat up and realized he lay on a hard stone floor, alone. He ran his fingers through the fine, soft hair on his head and his hand stopped on the edge of a pointed ear.

Startled, Larson leaped to his feet. He did not recognize his clothing: tight doeskin pants, a blue linen shirt, and a matching cape. "Wha?" he said stupidly. His hands clamped over both ears. Each came to a delicate point. "I'm a goddamn Vulcan!"

"Elf," said a voice. Larson whirled but saw no

one. Except for a belt and sword in the far corner, the room appeared empty.

Larson stared at his hands which looked smaller than he remembered. "Who are you?" he shouted. "Where are you?" If this was a Vietnamese torture, he found it extremely successful. He knew he had gone completely insane.

"Silence." The powerful voice echoed. "I am Freyr. You called me before you died."

"I did?" *Yes, I guess I did.* Larson caught a handful of the pale hair which fell to his shoulders. "Who am I?"

"I haven't time for foolishness," said the voice impatiently. "Neither have you. You've a purpose to fulfill."

Larson felt small and confused. "What purpose? Where am I? Help me please." He felt ridiculous pleading with a disembodied voice.

"Take up Valvitnir, your sword, and guard it well. Pass northward. You will find an old man and a young woman who are more than they seem. Trust them. They'll aid your task."

Larson's head whirled. "What task?"

No reply.

"Oh, hell." Larson walked to the corner. He hefted the swordbelt, a gaudily-tooled work of leather. He fastened it about his waist, and it dragged like dead weight at his side. Larson gazed at the ceiling. "Freyr? Freyr!"

Silence.

Larson patted the jewel-encrusted sword hilt. "I don't know how to use a sword!"

Nothing.

Larson shrugged. He pulled the worked steel from its sheath. The sleek blade glowed faintly blue. His unfamiliar hand fit the grip exactly. "Why me?"

He had not anticipated a reply. "I found it necessary to bridge time. We've few worshipers after the coming of the White Christ. Now, please go. Your companions will explain further."

Larson resheathed the sword and walked to the door. He took hold of its ring and pulled. It opened with a complaining creak to reveal a green meadow surrounded by hills. After months of artillery and jungle, the scene shocked Larson. Jaw gaping, he walked as if in a trance, and the door swung shut behind him.

The sun beamed down on Larson like a golden eye, striping the high grasses with light. In the distance, a tall patch of weeds rose like a tiny forest. Beyond, a real forest of evergreens waved like a chorus in the breeze. Anxiety balled in Larson's gut, and sweat beaded his neck. Fearful of the open terrain, he back-stepped and caught for the door handle. His fingers clawed through air. Startled anew, he whirled, staggered, and fell to the grass. Where the building had stood he saw nothing but fields, not even a shadow or a square of crushed foliage to indicate it had ever existed.

Larson rose to a crouch. *This cannot be real.* But the screams of his buddies echoed eerily through his memory, vividly clear. *If this is not a dream, then I am dead. And dead men cannot dream.* Without explanation for the bizarre series of events, Larson could do nothing but believe. He stood and stumbled forward, broad-based like a child learning to walk. Brownish grasses crunched beneath his boots. The sun formed an orange ball in the pale sky, but Larson could not guess whether morning aged or evening began.

His stride grew more confident as he headed for the stand of trees in the distance. He quelled an instinct to run. For now, the field seemed safe enough. He saw no need to incite enemies by crashing blindly through the meadow. The last few minutes seemed ridiculous to the point of impossibility. Yet, never having died before, Larson supposed he had no right to judge. *And if I am dead,* he surmised, *is this heaven or hell?* It seemed pretty enough. Lonely perhaps, but he had just begun exploring.

More curious than afraid, he trotted toward the higher grasses which he now recognized as cattails. The reeds bowed around a small pond which reflected the sky like an uncut sapphire. Without rations and slightly thirsty, he veered toward the water. Though he knew he could never have survived the guns in the jungle, he peered about him with caution. Until something came about to convince him more completely of his status as a corpse, or to prove there was no death after death, he saw no need to risk . . . whatever it was he had.

Larson frowned and abandoned his jumbled maze of thought. Despite his bold oratory in the jungle cabin, he'd never cared much for philosophy. And Vietnam taught even the most obsessive men to live moment by moment. He dropped to his stomach, gritted his teeth in anticipation, and wriggled among the cattails.

The surface of the pond spread before him, broken only by the ripples of wind and the wakes of water striders. For several seconds, Larson watched the insects glide like skaters, legs stretching like wires from their bulbous bodies. He touched the water, and it felt oddly chill after the enveloping heat of the jungles. Widening rings spread from his finger, lengthening his reflection. His gaze riveted on a face which seemed to stare from the bottom of the pond.

Larson recoiled with a cry. The face mimicked him with a perfection only nature could achieve. It was his reflection, yet the features were not at all as Larson remembered. His forehead was shorter, covered with bangs of fine, white hair. Larson had always felt self-conscious about the roundness of his "baby face." Now, it looked oval and angular, with high, sharp cheekbones and a narrow chin. His eyes seemed broadly-set, though he could not distinguish their color through the pond's distortion. He caught a lock of hair between his fingers. It was not actually white, but such a pale gold as to seem almost white. It reminded him of the color some women dyed their hair back in the States. He had never liked the unnatural, washed-out look, and had always been partial to brunettes.

Recalling his earlier discovery, Larson held the hair away from his head. He cocked his face sideways, and strained his eyes. The oddly-shaped ear remained just beyond his vision. He tried snapping his head about quickly, but found this even less successful. With a sigh, he resigned himself to a tactile impression of the ears. He rose to his full height and examined the clothing which had surprised him earlier. The cape flapped in the wind behind Larson, reminding him of a gripping scene from a Superman cartoon. The most striking feature of his garb was the sword at his left hip. Even sheathed in leather, it seemed to glow ever so slightly, like a television screen only recently shut off.

Larson turned his attention to his own stature.

He seemed as tall as ever, about six feet, but he had no way of knowing for certain. He looked thinner, too, and that bothered him. For a moment, he forgot he was lucky to have any body at all and cursed. Many painful hours had toned and shaped his muscles, now all gone to waste. He flexed an arm, and leaned closer to examine it. The sky darkened till only the sword remained clearly visible on the surface of the pond.

With a frown, Larson dropped to his haunches and waited for the cloud to pass. It did not. Slowly, the shadow encompassed the surface of the water and hovered there. Wary tension returned in a rush. Larson jerked his head upward. Swaying in the air above him was some enormous creature. Screaming, Larson leaped aside. A column of fire struck the water with a hiss.

Larson rolled to his feet as the creature banked for a second pass. He clawed at the cattails. Two bat-like wings carried a long, sleek body covered with scales the color of bark. Plates jutted from back and tail like a stegosaurus. It came around, and the sight of its triangular head mobilized Larson. He sprinted for the woods.

The beast caught him effortlessly, spraying the ground behind with flame. Panicked, Larson did not stop to wonder why the creature had such poor aim. The forest loomed closer, but still too far. His legs ached. Cold air rasped his lungs painfully and brought the taste of blood. Rationality returned only one thought to his numbed mind. *Among the trees, I can maneuver. It cannot.*

Heat seared the back of Larson's neck. Frantically, he ripped the cape from his shoulders and let the flaming linen drop to the ground. The beast rose over his head with a noise between a bark

and a human laugh. Larson ran on. He could not
control his thoughts, so he let them ramble as they
would. *Dragon. Goddamned fire-breathing dragon like
every legend and fairy tale I've ever read.* Yet there
was a major difference. This one was real.

A wall of trees rose before him. With a joyous
sob, Larson ran between them. Another man appeared suddenly before him, and Larson braked
with a sharp intake of breath. He stood, panting,
before the stranger while sweat dried on his back.
The other regarded him with scornful curiosity.
His features looked enough like the ones Larson
had seen in the pond to be those of a brother. Yet,
his hair and skin were as black as Larson's were
white. His eyes glowed a feral red.

"Dr-dr-dragon!" stuttered Larson, glad of the
stranger's company. "Run!"

The dark elf remained in Larson's path, un-
moving, like a carving in black onyx. He spoke in
a sibilant voice with an accent Larson recognized
but could not place. "Give me the sword."

Hope flared. *The sword.* "Certainly, if you can
use it." Larson's fingers trembled as he unsheathed
the sword and thrust it toward the stranger.

The dark elf withdrew with a high-pitched expletive. "On the ground, fool! Put it on the ground."

The words puzzled Larson. He balanced the
glowing blade on his hands and offered the hilt.
The sword vibrated slightly, and the light grew
brighter.

"On the ground, idiot!" The stranger retreated
farther. His voice lost some of its power.

The reaction raised Larson's suspicions. His mind
cleared, and he noticed the other elf as if for the
first time. At the Dark One's hip swung a black
wooden sheath from which jutted a hilt wrapped

with black split leather and garnished by red gemstones as wild as the stranger's eyes. *So why does he
want my sword?*

` The dark elf's lips twisted to a scowl. He took
one bold step forward and gestured angrily toward
the ground. Larson hesitated. They stood face to
face, dark to light, like chess queens before the
final battle. Larson caught the hilt of Valvitnir
in his callused palm. The stranger stiffened, and
sweat oozed above his drawn lips.

Larson knew he had the advantage with his
sword already freed. He would keep that upper
edge, at least until the dark elf realized he did not
know how to wield the blade. "Call me idiot, will
you?" said Larson, not at all certain it was not an
accurate assessment. Suddenly, six grueling weeks
of combat training seemed woefully inadequate.
He executed an awkward fencing lunge. The sword
whined like a hungry dog. The dark elf cursed
and vanished as completely as the building in the
fields.

Larson basked in his triumph for scant seconds.
Flame gouted through the trees with a heat that
made him scream. Despite the forest, the dragon's
aim seemed to have improved miraculously. Still
clutching the sword, Larson ran, dodging trees
with a speed born of desperation. Behind he heard
a beastly roar of frustration, followed by the whisk
of giant wings as the creature rose above the forest.

Branches rustled overhead, too loud for wind.
Fire lanced before him in a column, but the tree-
tops obscured the dragon's vision. Sparks bounced
outward from the impact and died among the
greenery. Larson ran in random circles, doubling
back like a fox. But the creature followed his
ruses, apparently by sound. Soon, the maneuvers

wore on the elf, and his run slowed dangerously.
The stabbing fires came closer, threatening to set
the entire forest ablaze.

In the distance, Larson saw a more benign fire,
the flickering orange of a camp. Desperate, he ran
toward it. As he neared, he observed a single
figure hunched before it with back turned. From
the short gray hair, Larson supposed it was an
elderly man and instantly regretted steering the
dragon toward the stranger. Too tired to swerve,
he ran on.

The man rose and turned suddenly, confirming
Larson's impression. Though clean-shaven, the
man's lined face revealed his age and gave him an
air of power. He wore a loose-fitting yellow gar-
ment, trimmed with black and belted at the waist.
Two swords girded his waist, a matched set slightly
curved like an old Japanese katana and shoto.
Gold brocade enhanced both hilts. But the feature
which drew Larson's attention was a wooden staff
at the old man's feet. Its tip was carved like a claw,
and the four black-nailed toes cradled a sapphire.

Flame shot through the spruce, and a wall of
heat knocked Larson to one knee at the edge of
camp. "Dragon!" He screamed his warning though
his lungs felt raw. "Fire . . . breathing . . . dragon!"

The older man seemed unperturbed. "As far as
I know they all spit fire." He smiled encouragingly.

From the ground, Larson stared at the stranger's baggy yellow pants. He raised his head to a
sagging face. The old man's eyes were brown,
slightly slanted, and with prominent epicanthic
folds. New danger lent Larson a second wind. He
lurched to his feet and reached instinctively for
the gun which no longer lay slung across his
shoulder.

The stranger watched his antics with obvious amusement. "Beast won't come to ground and fight fair? We'll see what we can do about it." He winked.

Larson fought for breath, quelling panic. He was no longer in Nam. An Oriental face was nothing to fear in and of itself, though he wondered why he should find such a face in Old Scandinavia, or dragons for that matter.

The stranger seemed to notice none of Larson's consternation. He strode past the campfire where the trees thinned and undergrowth grew lush in the sunlight. Larson felt more comfortable despite the open terrain and the dragon shadow which darkened the weeds. The forest seemed much more like those of the New Hampshire camp he had known in his youth than the Vietnamese tangles of stench and death. He followed.

"Wyrm!" screamed the old man.

Larson cringed back as the dragon descended. Its breath reeked of ozone, and scales rattled together like shingles. The beast's jaws gaped. Its black fangs were like giant stalactites, and Larson dodged the globs of spittle which struck the ground with a smoky hiss. With a whoop of wild joy, the old man pulled a piece of metal from his belt and hurled it toward the bus-sized target. His hand was a blur as he pitched three more missiles at the dragon. The first glanced from the hoary chest plates. The second struck, and an explosion rocked the trees. Flame gouted and spread across the dragon, engulfing it. The huge body plummeted with an unearthly wail.

Instinct flattened Larson to the ground; his heart pounded like gunshot. Smoke burned his eyes, and fumes choked him. As he watched through a veil of mist, the smoldering corpse faded to memory. Two of the metallic missiles thumped to earth, and the old man gathered them with a curse. Larson wanted to speak. His lips parted, but no words came forth. He rose, gathered scattered wits, and tried to understand how Freyr expected him to survive with only a sword in a world with both dragons and grenades. All courage fled his overtaxed mind. No amount of field drills could have prepared him for such a madman's reality. He stood utterly still, hoping to escape his fever dreams, yet equally afraid he might again awaken in the jungles.

The old man approached and bowed courteously. "I've not had such fun in days. I, Kensei Gaelinar, thank you, hero." He bowed again.

"Kensei Gaelinar?" Larson's Bronx accent mangled the name. He extended his hand in greeting, but quickly withdrew it when the old man showed no recognition of the gesture. Muddled, he continued. "Um . . . I'm Al." His name seemed pitiably inadequate, so he added inanely ". . . er . . . um . . ."

"Allerum." Gaelinar's brows knitted together in thought. "Odd name. Elven, I suppose. I haven't seen many of your kind in Midgard." He gestured toward the fire. "You look hungry, Allerum. Would you join us?"

More intrigued by the old man's use of the plural pronoun than the misinterpretation of his name, Larson quickly scanned the brush. He saw no one. The odor of roasting meat rose from the campfire and made his stomach rumble. Glad for human company, Larson followed his host to the fire where four steaks hung from a spit. Forgotten in the excitement, their lower sides were vastly overcooked.

"Loki's children!" swore the Kensei. He dismantled the spit and slid the blackened carcasses onto a piece of leather on the dirt. He speared a hunk of meat with a sharpened stick and passed it to Larson apologetically. "I'm not the best cook."

As adrenalin ebbed, Larson found himself ravenously hungry. Saliva poured into his mouth like the rich juices which sizzled on the lesser cooked areas of the steak. He did not know what sort of meat he had accepted from his Oriental-looking companion, but the aching void of his gut would have been pleasured even by manflesh were it the staple of this strange world.

Gaelinar answered his unspoken question. "It's the last of the fresh venison. We smoked the rest for the journey ahead."

Gaelinar used "we" again, Larson noted. *Does the old man simply refer to himself in this odd manner?* Larson had not seen any living creature to dispute his conclusion, except the dark elf he had encountered at the edge of the woods. The thought made him shiver, and so he discarded it. The meat did taste a lot like the deer he used to shoot in the upstate forests, though, perhaps because of his hunger, he found the flavor richer despite the ash.

"Where do you come from, elf?" Kensei Gaelinar asked around a mouthful.

Reluctantly, Larson lowered the food to answer. "I come from far, far away." He winced. His words were not only trite, but grossly understated.

Gaelinar raised his eyebrows encouragingly, but Larson lapsed into silence. His teeth ripped muscle and gristle indiscriminately from the preboned feast. But when the growls of his stomach settled to a satisfied purr, Larson grew more curious about his new companion. "Those . . . um . . . missiles of yours saved my life. How do they work?"

Gaelinar's elbow fell to his knee; his sharpened stick still supported a ring of meat. His slanted eyes slitted, and his features twisted to a scowl of withering disdain. "Your sword didn't help much either."

Larson settled back gingerly, and his chest flinched taut beneath his tunic. He tried to remember what he'd said which might have angered the Kensei. "P-please, I . . . I meant no disrespect," he stuttered.

Gaelinar met Larson's eyes, and his expression went from affronted to puzzled. As suddenly, he smiled. "Oh! You think . . ." He laughed. "No, no, hero. Magic, not my shuriken, flamed that dragon."

Magic. The explanation seemed embarrassingly obvious and oddly comforting. For reasons Larson could not understand, sorceries seemed far more benign than grenades. Unexpectedly, visions from Vietnam flared, horrific as nightmares. He remembered sitting in darkness complete save for the narrow slit of moon over the rows of grass huts. A dank wind rustled the barracks, blended chorus with the shriek of insects and the gentle whisper of sentries at the fire base gate. *Peaceful.* For a moment he could almost forget the ubiquitous threat of the V.C. who owned the jungle nights.

Back pressed to the door jamb of his hut, Larson lifted a joint to his lips; its tip was a singular bobbing light in the pitch darkness. He inhaled. Smoke rolled across his tongue leaving a sweet taste, then funneled into his lungs. He squeezed his mouth shut and held it, swallowing gently. *Nothing could spoil the sanctity of this night.*

A flash of red-orange light colored the sky and outlined the bamboo of huts on either side. Even as Larson's mind responded to the sight, an explosion rocked his foundation, filling his head with sound. Something unseen thudded against his cheek, spinning his face with the force of a slap.

With a warning cry, Larson crashed through the door of his hut. Static blattered and a muffled voice screamed. "Incoming fire! Incoming . . ." A second mortar blast rendered the words incomprehensible. Larson collided with a man in the entranceway with a force which wrenched his ankle. Pain lanced through his abdomen, and Fisher's baritone cursed him with steamy epithets only a street kid could design. As Larson dived for his bunk and the M-16 on the quilt, two more men pushed past and out the door.

The explosion had torn a hole in the hut, and the harried exits of Larson's companions through the door seemed as ludicrous as the gunshot at the fire base perimeter. Not content to lie low while mortars shattered the camp to chaos, soldiers wasted round after round shooting blindly into the jungle. With a sigh, Larson seized his gun to help, but a roaring mortar lit a scene which froze him in place. Danny lay face down on the floor, unresponsive to Tom Dragelin's frantic proddings.

Larson leaped forward, pulled Dragelin's arm with a force that sent the other man reeling against his bunk. Dragelin protested furiously, but Larson flipped Danny over. The body rolled like a rag doll. Blood slicked Larson's fingers, and he recoiled with a choked sob. A chunk of wood from the cottage foundation was embedded in Danny's chest like a stake. His glazed eyes glared accusingly in the scarlet glow of the mortars. The continuous stream of gunshot, screamed orders, man-shouts, and the louder, broken reports of mortars blended to a numbing, unrecognizable ring.

Dragelin's quavering voice was the only thing Larson heard. "Is he. . . ?" They had seen death before, too many times in this sordid movie without beginning or end. But this was Danny, and this was different.

Larson dared not feel for a pulse. "Help me carry him."

He caught Danny behind the shoulders, waited until Dragelin seized the legs, and they lifted together. Danny sagged between them, dead weight, yet they struggled through milling soldiers toward the infirmary.

A roar rose wildly above the rest. The high-pitched scream of jets slammed against Larson's ear drums. He grimaced against the agony of sound, unable to clamp burdened hands to his ears. Then the noise dulled to a long thunder roll. He caught a glimpse of two red disks in the sky, like feral eyes. Abruptly, the jungle flamed in a wide circle. Mercifully, the mortar fire ceased. The answering call of guns died to the last panicked bursts, and the sour odor of napalm pinched his nose. Long after, the screams of the dying echoed through his dreams.

Larson's mind returned to the present with a start. His fists were clenched against sweat which ran like blood. His every nerve felt taut. Adrenalin coursed, warm, through his veins. The face which stared curiously into his own was Oriental, yet rounder than a Vietnamese visage. The eyes were the yellow-brown of ancient pages, and they held an odd power which reminded Larson of a picture in a book his mother had read to him as a child. The book was a juvenile rendition of the stories of King Arthur; the drawing was of Merlin the Magician.

"Are you all right, hero?" asked Gaelinar with concern.

"Yes," responded Larson without conviction. Realization struck a cruel blow. Back home, technology made men equals. Here power stemmed from skill with sword or sorcery, and he possessed neither. One thing he knew, he wanted to remain in the graces of a man who could flame dragons to ash. "Forgive my ignorance. I'm grateful for your magic which saved my life. As a . . ." He rummaged for a word. Warlock seemed derogatory, wizard too plain. Sorcerer conjured images of Mickey Mouse juggling buckets of water and an animated broom. Magician reminded him of staged card tricks. ". . . great and wonderful user of magics . . ." The term seemed vague enough for safety. ". . .you might understand my problem. I'm from another world."

To Larson, his explanation seemed anything but humorous, yet the Kensei's features cracked a smile. Between them, light flashed, bright as a search flare. Larson staggered back with a cry. His eyes snapped shut against the glare, and red spots winked on the backs of his eyelids. He opened them hurriedly, not certain what to expect and, so, prepared for nothing. What he saw shocked him dumb. A woman stood between him and Gaelinar, more starkly real than anything he had experienced since death. She was beautiful in a way Larson could not have understood before he glimpsed her.

Plagued by a passion that native whores could never satisfy, any white woman would have seemed more than human to Larson. Yet it was not simply heightened sexual tension which made this woman inhumanly desirable. She was slim beneath a baggy gray robe which in no way marred the perfect arcs of hips and breasts. Her skin looked snowy white. Her eyes echoed Gaelinar's power, bitter gray as gale-tossed surf. Her hair fell to midback in a gold-white cascade, a color Larson had always hated for its artificiality. Now it became his favorite hue. Dyed or real did not matter, it belonged to the woman whose smile, Larson felt, would satisfy him for weeks.

She did smile. Though tinged with sarcasm, her words plied Larson like song. "Oh, please, great mage Gaelinar. Enlighten us with more of your sorceries." The sapphire gleamed in the staff at the Kensei's feet.

The old man rose with a stiffly formal bow. "Lord Allerum, I think it best you meet the Lady Silme, Dragonrank of Sapphire Claw. I shall take neither credit nor blame for her magics."

"Uh . . . hi," said Larson, instantly cursing the bumbling stupidity which had characterized his every action since this day began. From the towel-cracking days of junior high to the raw jibes of boot camp, he had tried to appear competent. Death, it seemed, had shaken his confidence. He tried again. "Lady Silme." He mimicked Gaelinar's bow. "It is my very best pleasure to meet you." *Not bad for my first attempt at courtly talk,* Larson rewarded himself with nonverbal praise.

"You owe me a shuriken, witch," said Gaelinar with none of Larson's respect. "Your fireworks destroyed it. I could have taken the beast without you."

Amusement left Silme's features, replaced by a concern which lined her face beyond its years. "Silence, swordlord." For a brief moment she grinned again at the awkward sound of his title. "You speak as if dragons are commonplace. Someone of Dragonrank summoned the creature."

Gaelinar spoke with bitterness. "Bramin?"

"I recognized his power."

The Kensei paced around the campfire. Silme took the seat he had abandoned and speared a venison steak with a stick. Larson watched both, contemplating a means to correct their misunderstanding of his name without making himself, or Gaelinar, look foolish.

Gaelinar mumbled. "He's close then?"

Silme nodded as she gnawed the meat.

"And the elf?" Gaelinar indicated Larson with a subtle toss of his head.

Silme shrugged. She regarded Larson with a mixture of curiosity and suspicion.

Larson remained silent, not certain what she expected from him. A memory surfaced in his mind with the intensity of a new idea. *You will find an old man and a young woman who are more than they seem. . . . Your companions will explain further.* "You two!" he called triumphantly. "Freyr said you'd tell me about my task."

Gaelinar stopped. Silme blinked in the waning light. "Freyr?"

Larson picked up the pacing where Gaelinar left off. "Yes, Freyr, or at least his voice. I . . ." He broke off, realizing he must sound as touched as the lieutenant who swore he had met Jesus Christ among other raving blasphemies and was duly shipped home. The strained glances between his new companions came not wholly unexpectedly. Further clarification would only place his sanity more completely in doubt. "So you don't know my task?"

Silme returned her attention to the meal while Kensei Gaelinar shook his head slowly. "I'm afraid not."

"Shit." Larson sat, head cradled in his palms. "How many remarkable old men and young women can there be?" Yet he had no way of answering the question. If his experiences to date gave any indication, this world was crowded with extraordinary people.

Silme and Gaelinar offered no comfort. As the sky dimmed to gray, they turned to matters more relevant to themselves. Larson brooded in silence, thinking they had forgotten him. The setting sun colored the horizon with flame-colored arches, a doorway for the daring. Idly, he wondered if he could pass through it like a gate and find himself home or in Oz or back in the stinking hell of Vietnam.

After a time, Silme turned from her companion, retrieved her sapphire-tipped staff, and approached Larson. She moved with a dancer's confident grace, but her eyes shifted in the manner of a deer. Larson stared, surprised at how, despite death and the oddities of his new surroundings, her beauty excited him.

Silme stopped several yards from Larson. Her features remained soft, but she jabbed the tip of her staff toward him. Her words emerged as a calculated threat. "Are you who you claim?"

Her tone made Larson uneasy. He shifted to a crouch. "Y-yes, of course," he stammered defensively, immediately realizing his hasty reply robbed him of any opportunity to correct her misunderstanding of his name. Thrust into a new life and a strange world, he supposed he needed a new identity. Allerum was not the name he would have chosen, but it would do as well as any other. "At least as close as could be expected. You see, I . . ."

Silme interrupted. "And your purpose in the world of Midgard?"

Larson fidgeted. His gaze swept the tree line. *She knows I'm from another world. How?* But the answer came to him as swiftly as the question. He sifted his thoughts for the duller cosmology of his mythology text. The Vikings believed in nine worlds, each inhabited by its own race of creatures: giants, gods, elves, dwarves. *Midgard,* Larson recalled, *was the land of men. To her, I'm an elf.* The thought seemed foreign. *In that respect, I am from another world.*

"Your purpose?" Silme prompted.

Larson had forgotten her question. "I'm on a mission. My, um, commander informed me I would find an older man and a young woman who could explain things further. I'm afraid I've mixed you up with someone else."

Silme scowled, unsatisfied. "What connection do you have with Bramin?"

The word meant nothing to Larson. "What's a Bramin?"

Anger darkened Silme's eyes. "I won't stand for lies! Do you think me stupid enough to believe coincidence placed an elf in a wash of Bramin's magic, playing with a conjured dragon?"

"Playing!"

Soundlessly, Gaelinar cleared the distance to Silme and caught her arm. "It wouldn't be the first time an innocent stumbled into Bramin's designs against your life."

Silme never took her gaze from Larson. "An elf?"

Gaelinar shrugged. "We've come upon stranger occurrences."

Silme raised her brows and eyed her Oriental companion. "An elf?"

Gaelinar sighed. "In Lord Allerum's defense, the dragon seemed less than friendly toward him. You swore to protect mankind from Bramin's wrath. Would you deny wardings to a traveler without bedding or rations because he happens to be an elf? Shame on you, lady." He smiled at Larson. "Join us for the night?" He motioned to a pile of furs near the campfire.

Silme opened her mouth to protest, but Gaelinar waved her silent. "If the elf can slay us in our sleep, he deserves to wear our heads at his belt." Respectfully, he bowed toward Silme then turned and knelt in the furs. He tapped a space at his side invitingly.

Larson hesitated, sorting his fears. Gaelinar's camaraderie beckoned, despite his features. Silme's comeliness seemed added incentive; he found her aloofness a challenge. He felt certain from their display of power against the dragon, that either of his new acquaintances could already have killed him if they had wished. He turned a glance toward Silme.

Silme's eyes met Larson's stare. She smiled weakly. "Gaelinar's right, of course. You may join us for the night." She emphasized the last phrase as if to assure herself of the transience of his presence.

Larson rose and paced to the furs by the fire. He sprawled beside Gaelinar, more comfortable for soft bedding and warmth. Silme stood, watching the two men, arms spread. Her gaze seemed to pass through and beyond them. Her eyes blazed like gemstones.

"What's she doing?" Larson asked, concerned.

"Quiet," whispered Gaelinar. "You'll mar the spell."

Larson fell silent. He watched in fascination as the grim lines in Silme's face deepened. Light streamed from each hand, the dazzling white of phosphorus. Snakelike, the beams coiled around the camp and met halfway. Blue light welled to life on her fingers, wound about the white with an intensity that colored stars and moon. Silme stepped forward and examined her efforts briefly. At an approving nod, the enchantments faded, but Larson still felt the presence of their brooding power. Protected by the sorceress' wards, Larson pondered the coming day until fatigue overtook him and granted a dreamless sleep.

CHAPTER 2

Manslayer

"The belief in a supernatural source of evil is not necessary; men alone are quite capable of every wickedness."
—Joseph Conrad,
Under Western Eyes

A yellow edge of sun tipped over the horizon, chasing darkness in bands of blue and pink. As if it were a signal, the sleepers within the sorceress' wards stirred. Silme was first to open her eyes and greet the dawn, but her movements wakened Gaelinar and Larson. Her enchantments had dwindled through the night, yet when Larson tried to leave the protected circle to relieve himself, he discovered they still held the potency of an electric fence.

Silme snickered and dispelled her magics with a word. Gaelinar bowed politely. "Lord Allerum, we've enjoyed your company, but we must move along and you as well."

"Wait." Silme rummaged through a weathered pack, pulled out a bag of woven cloth, and handed it to the elf. "Rations," she explained. "I noticed

you carried none and couldn't leave you starving."
She clipped her words short as if to register her
disapproval. "You must have left someplace in an
awful hurry." Her tone demanded explanation.

Larson declined to answer. The few times he
had tried to enlighten his new friends had put his
sanity in question. He preferred an aura of mys-
tery to one of lunacy. "I thank you both." He
extended a hand, hoping Silme might accept it
like a royal maiden in the movies. He would gladly
submit to the ridicule of an entire platoon if it
meant a chance to kiss her fingers. But Silme
showed no more understanding of the gesture
than Gaelinar had of his attempted handshake.

After a breakfast of dried meat and fruit, Larson took his leave. He skirted the tangled clearing,
reminded of Vietnam's towering elephant grasses
which forced the point man to waddle as he cleared
a path for his followers. He traveled northward,
beneath interlocking branches which muted the
sun. Pines flowed endlessly past, lower branches
withered in the shadow of their younger brothers.
Songbirds flitted above Larson's head, their sweet
trills a welcome relief from the too-well remembered screams of macaws.

Near midday, his mood reversed. He began to
question Silme's and Gaelinar's sidelong glances in
the clearing and the sorceress' mistrustful queries.
The birds became less apparent, their song more
shrill. A squirrel, startled from its food hunt,
scolded, while Larson was still some distance away.
A shiver traversed him from buttocks to neck,
warning of imminent peril. Repeatedly, Larson
reminded himself this forest hid no snipers. But
his fear remained and intensified nearly to panic

until he would have bet all the water in his pouch that unseen eyes watched from the branches.

Larson stopped, hoping the sudden cessation of his own passage would amplify any noises around him. The harsh call of a crow ruined the silence. Suddenly, light sparked before him, flaring to blinding brilliance. He dropped to a crouch, now capable enough to recognize a sorcerer's craft. Desire dared him to hope the power originated from the slim-waisted beauty he had left that morning.

But the figure which sprang to clarity was cloaked in a blackness which was echoed in his features. Red eyes met Larson's for the second time, filled with cruelty and misplaced hatred. This time, the dark elf clutched a staff like Silme's, but the gem gripped between carven claws was a flawless diamond. And he raised it threateningly.

Shaken, Larson stumbled two steps backward. His mind reverberated with memory of his last encounter with the demon elf. His trembling fingers found the hilt of his sword and drew it with a rasp of steel.

"Fool!" Bramin's voice mocked him. "Do you think your toy will save you from my wrath?" He suffixed his threat with a single coarse syllable.

Pain lanced through Larson's fist, flaming to an agony which swept his entire arm. The sword fell from his weakened grip and crashed against stone with a shower of ice blue sparks. Bramin's assault continued ruthlessly. Waves of torture racked mind and body, twitched Larson's limbs like those of a stringless marionette. Scream after scream ripped from his raw lungs in ghastly duet with Bramin's laughter.

Pain stabbed through Larson's body like daggers, worse than any agony described as hell. Could he have uttered a coherent sentence, he would have pleaded for death. But Bramin knew no mercy. His spell stole strength of body and reserves of mind, seared like flame, and convulsed its hapless victim with anguish.

Suddenly, the pain stopped. Larson flopped to the ground like a beached fish. His mind jumped erratically. His breaths came thankfully easier from his aching lungs. Through vision clouded by his ordeal, he saw movement, and watched the blue blur of the sword slide toward Bramin's gesturing hand. He understood what was happening, but it meant nothing to him. *Let the dark elf have the sword. I have no use for it.*

The shadows flickered, suffused with blue as the sword flared with an anger all its own. The hilt knocked against a stone in its path toward Bramin, splattering enchantments like the rays of a star. A soft breaking of brush from behind startled Larson where he lay helpless and still, recalling stories of injured soldiers left for dead. Silver flashed over his head, casting a slight breeze which cooled his tortured limbs.

Bramin recoiled with a pained hiss. As he clamped his hands to his chest, his red eyes blazed purple with rage. His link with the sword broke, and it halted with a lurch. Blood trickled between his fingers, and his slim hand raised in an ominous gesture. Larson recognized a shaped piece of steel jutting from Bramin's wound. The dark elf's gaze locked on the gold-robed Kensei behind Larson who had hurled the shuriken.

Sorceries crackled, bounced between Bramin's outstretched hands as though they were opposing mirrors, and intensified to blinding white. Bramin moved. His magic leaped like a beast and screamed

toward the man behind Larson. Larson heard a
curse. Then, a second jagged ray sprang from the
brush. Magics met with a sound like thunder, and
both spells broke to glittering traces. *Silme!* Larson
shielded his eyes against the backlash.

Bramin's malevolent voice broke the ensuing
silence. "Hel take all your souls!" The diamond in
his staff winked black, and the dark elf vanished.

Gaelinar's callused hand gripped Larson's upper arm and hoisted the elf to his feet. Movement
dizzied Larson. He staggered, but regained his
balance with the Kensei's aid. His stomach heaved.
Unable to avoid the inevitable, Larson ripped free,
dropped to his knees, and vomited with an intensity unknown since more experienced soldiers had
forced him to wallow through rotting bodies to
prepare him for death. Embarrassment brought
tears to his eyes. He knew the most beautiful woman
in existence watched, surely with disgust.

But Silme waited until Larson's sickness passed
and squeezed his hand with a reassurance which
almost made the ordeal worthwhile. "My humblest
apologies, Lord Allerum," she said. "Had I known
we shared such an enemy, I would never have let
you travel alone."

Larson bowed though his legs felt weak and
rubbery. He chose his words with delicate care.
"Lady, I could never hold any offense against
you." He beamed at his own efforts.

Gaelinar continued. "We dared not trust you.
Light elves act as capricious as Bramin's kind do
evil." He gestured, toward the place where the
dark elf had stood. "But faery creatures of any
sort are rare in the manworld of Midgard. We
assumed you were outcast, that Alfheim's lord,

Freyr, had exiled you. Bramin's attack and your sword tell us otherwise."

Larson tried to recall his readings on the subject of elves. He had concentrated his interest on gods and war, and all he could dredge from memory was the respective good and evil tendencies of light and dark elves. He had read somewhere that tales of the latter were so rare many authorities believed dark elves and dwarves to be interchangeable. He regarded Silme and Gaelinar. *I have to trust someone. With enemies as unassailable as Bramin and his dragons, I have no chance of survival without capable, knowledgeable companions. And these two people have already rescued me twice.* "This may sound strange or impossible . . ." He spoke slowly, studying Silme's face for any clue he might have overstepped the boundaries of credibility. "Freyr called me from a place beyond the scope of your nine worlds. Aside from a few legends, I'm ignorant of even the simplest matters of Midgard."

Silme's face twisted in doubt, but her eyes widened and her lips pursed in consideration. Her gaze dropped to the faintly-glowing sword on the ground, and her expression changed suddenly to one of surprise. Ignoring Larson's revelation, she knelt before Valvitnir.

Larson cleared his throat. "Why are elves so uncommon here?"

Gaelinar seemed to accept Larson's explanation easily. "Travel between the nine worlds requires great effort and power. Even the gods cannot wholly disregard the energy such travel demands. Elves of any sort were never common. In time, men grew to despise the dark elves for their cruelty and vile sense of humor. Where men still remember dark elves, they slay them on sight.

"Light elves view men as narrow-minded beings so concerned with death they refuse to enjoy their short lives. Man's somber nature made light elves extremely uncomfortable, so they gradually curtailed all commerce with the world of men. Now, the tales and memories of elves have been confused or, at best, forgotten. At times, dark elves are welcomed because of the legends of light elves, and light elves are slain for the ancient crimes of their dark cousins. Mostly, the sidelong glances and whispered comments which follow any stranger viewed as different will accompany you throughout the world of Midgard."

Silme's voice seemed distant as she returned the blade to its sheath at Larson's side. "That sword is the work of a pure and powerful god. I don't know its abilities or purpose, but assuredly they will shape the destiny of our world." Her features assumed the intensity of her words. "Magic saps the life force of the one who calls it forth. Understand this, Allerum, a god paid dearly for your quest."

Guilt preyed on Larson's conscience. *Does Silme know how easily I gave up the struggle to Bramin, that I would have tossed him the sword to avoid his wrath?* But the situation had changed. Quest or no, Bramin's cruelty charged Larson to seek revenge.

The three continued north and east through forest which seemed endless. Pine passed to more pine, like the recurrent background of a cartoon until Larson began to believe they had gained no ground since the confrontation. But the walk gave him the chance to ask many questions. Their answers gave the world a logical order, magic aside. There were villages and governments, monarchies, and temples to the Northern gods. Wizards were a rarity, despite Larson's run-in with two of Midgard's most powerful on his first day.

"Most men," Silme told him, "become farmers or artisans. Those with interest in sword or bow join armies or sell their services as bodyguards, soldiers, and assassins. To become a sorcerer requires an innate ability and a lifetime dedicated to magic. Even then, only those few stamped with 'the mark' can attain the power of Dragonrank." She displayed her right hand, and Larson stared at the claw-shaped scar which marred her skin.

As they walked, Silme and Gaelinar schooled Larson concerning travel foods and horse trading. They introduced him to the most common monetary system of the Northern kingdoms. But it was Bramin's name which opened a veritable flood of explanation, and Silme talked of the half-elf throughout the evening and on through a dinner of smoked venison.

"A warped creature," Silme described her half brother. ". . . twisted by a legacy base as demon shadow and intent on inappropriate retribution since I scarce passed from glass level to semiprecious." She indicated the sapphire which glimmered at the tip of her staff. "Bramin leagued with Loki the Evil One." Her voice grated with dissent, as if mere mention of the name caused her pain. "So, I joined with Vidarr the Silent, a god whose strength is exceeded only by that of the thunderlord, Thor. Even then, I knew someone must stop Bramin before his vengeance harmed innocents."

She took a bite of meat, eyes distant. Larson longed to put his arms around her and offer comfort, but Gaelinar sat between them. Her voice grew stronger. "Bramin held three years of ad-

vantage over me. He swept through the Dragonranks like wildfire in a shipyard. I knew I could
never equal his training, but I fought to follow.
Nearly every spell I chose to learn could be used
as a defense against one of his. I forsook many of
my own offenses for wards against him, a vast
repertoire of counterspells as protection for Bramin's victims."

Silme's eyes remained fierce points of blue, but
her body sagged as if with fatigue. "He left the
school at the rank of Master. Though three grades
behind, I followed, hoping to withhold his evils
from the world. Kensei Gaelinar nearly equals the
odds between us."

Larson could think of nothing to say in the
awesome wake of her story. He let his mind ab-
sorb the oddities of Midgard as the meal continued in silence and night plunged the forest into
darkness.

At the base of the deepest root of the World
Tree lay the Spring of Hvergelmir which fed the
rivers of the world and was in turn filled by them.
Its waters frothed like the boiling brew in a witch's
cauldron. On its bank stood two figures, one light
with a rotted core, the other wholly dark.

Bramin's life aura spread about him like flame.
His voice was gritty with accusation. "You never
warned me the sword was warded. I shudder to
imagine the damage had I taken it in hand. Retrieve your own blade."

Hvergelmir belched putrid gas. Loki regarded
his prodigy with wry amusement. "Relax, Hatespawn. I didn't know. It wasn't warded when it was
still in my hands." He smiled at some private joke.
"But your efforts will not go for naught. This task

is so important, I offer reward without equal. Should you retrieve Valvitnir, you shall have the hand of my daughter, Hel, and rulership of her realm."

Bramin paused, momentarily speechless. His aura flickered and dulled to pink as anger faded. As Helmaster, he would be lord of the dead; the souls of men would become his to rack and rend through eternity.

Loki read his thoughts, and spoke over Hvergel-mir's gurglings. "Beyond eternity, Hatespawn. If we destroy that sword, the nine worlds shall become ours. All men and gods will topple, lost to a chaos only you and I control. Not even the Fates can stay our vengeance."

Loki's enthusiasm spread to the sorcerer. "I've a plan," called Bramin as he watched lines of bub-bles rise from the boiling spring. "In the woods, I did a mind search. Freyr's champion is a human in elf guise, a man from the future and a poor choice. The true structure of Midgard makes such knowledge as he has obsolete, and he has none of the mental protections of our kind. In short, he understands nothing of the sword's power and will fall easy prey to illusion. Although," he added bitterly. "Silme's presence makes my task infinitely more difficult."

Loki paced, distressed. It seemed almost too easy.

Bramin's next revelation redirected his thoughts. "I can read the runes," he said softly. His sword scraped from its ebony sheath, and its writings gleamed to vivid relief:

Helblindi
The Sword of Darkness
All who die on its edge
Add their souls to Hel's shadow hordes.
Their screams shall echo to Valhalla's barred gate.

Loki smiled. "And now you know why brave men must fear it. By assuring them eternity in the hall of men who succumb to illness or cowardice, we strip all glory from death in battle." *And add strength to my own army at the final battle,* he gloated in silence.

Bramin's fist clenched with purpose. "The writings are clear," the dark elf reminded Loki of his promise. "My vengeance?"

The burbling waters seemed to join Loki's laughter. "When you bring the sword, you shall have them many times over. But if petty slayings amuse you in the meantime, enjoy them. Just don't let them interfere with your task."

Bramin's malignant smile was his only answer.

Larson dreamed. He saw his sword, Valvitnir, gleaming blue as muted porch light. It spun in his hands, flinging glimmers in wild arcs. Gradually, the scene faded to a vivid view of the pine forest. He wandered wonderingly through a world of green highlights as tree trunks shuddered around him and their branches fused to a common core.

The whole seemed not unlike an insect, a giant, hairy spider, amusingly awkward. The trees rose like legs, moved from the confines of the forest, and Larson followed curiously. Eleven trunks gave the creature mobility, each with a name that ran through his mind like the players on a team: Svol, Gunnthra, Fjorm, Fimbulthul, Slidr, Hrid, Sylgr, Ylgr, Vid, Leiptr, and Gjoll. Even as he repeated the strange-sounding names, they muted.

The forest became a valley whose darkness the moon could not graze. The spider's legs split the blackness as they transformed into streams which sparkled like diamonds. They no longer towered up from the ground. Their waters plunged downward to meet a swirling torrent, a glorious cascade of foam unmatched by any work of man. Mesmerized, the dream-Larson worked the sword from its sheath and watched the tumescent waters wink shadows through the glow of the sword's magic. He drew back his arm and hurled the blade. The sword tumbled end over end. It hit the burbling spring with a splash and sank instantly out of sight.

Even as relief rushed to replace the urgency of his quest, the illusion acquired the frightening quality of his unbidden memory of Danny's death. An unfamiliar obscenity crossed his thoughts briefly. The scene wavered. The spring flushed to the color of blood, and bloated, white bodies gorged the streams. An alien presence knocked his consciousness askew.

He awoke screaming. Gentle hands first caught his wrists and then drew his face to a chest which muffled his cries. Consciousness changed his screams to sobs, and his tears made the thin gray cloth cling to Silme's breasts. She rocked him, humming as if to a child, oblivious to the turmoil in Larson's soul. He ached, loosing tears held far too long, tears he had locked away as war forced him from the mischievous antics of adolescence to the atrocities of men. These were the tears he'd never shed for Danny.

"Are you all right? What happened?" Silme asked in a voice which could soothe a stampede.

"Just a dream," Larson heard himself say, though he made no effort to speak. "Just a bad nightmare." His own voice brought a new rush of sorrow. "Oh, Jesus, what's wrong with me?"

Silme pulled her fingers from Larson's hair with

a crackle of static. She seized both of his hands, squatted before him, and met his gaze. "What was the dream?"

Overwhelmed by the intensity of the sorceress' gaze, Larson closed his eyes. Tears pooled on his lashes, and he spoke around his sobs with gritted teeth. "I'm sorry. Let me pull myself together first." For a brief moment, he hated this woman who was callous enough to stare at a broken man. But when he raised his lids, the sincerity of her pained expression moved him to pity. He let the tears fall where they might and began to relate his dream.

Larson told Silme and Gaelinar of the forest and its strange conformation. He described the eleven streams and their source and was surprised to find he remembered their names. His narrative slowed as he recalled tossing the sword into the burbling spring and the relief inspired by its sacrifice. Even as Larson detailed the final sequence, memory battered against his sanity. He held his gaze on Silme, aware a single glimpse of Gaelinar's slanted eyes would snap his control over the flashbacks.

"There's more." Silme would allow no denial. "Something frightened you."

The tears slackened to a trickle. Larson shook his head with an intensity that whipped his face with hair. "The dream ends there. The rest is . . ." he sneaked a look at Gaelinar, then closed his eyes tight against dizziness, ". . . just recollections of horrors I've seen."

Silme pounced on his words without mercy. "For some reason, your mind relates them to this dream. Tell me . . ."

"No!" The word came out more like a whine

than a command. Larson sagged forward on his
bedding. His tears discolored the furs in a pool.
*How can I tell Silme about a world where technology
makes equals of the foolish and the skilled? How can I
describe a place where there are no heroes or villains,
where the lines between good and evil blur to interpretation, where men rape and torture innocents in the name
of justice.* Larson slumped to one elbow, unable to
face his new companions. *How can I expect her to
understand the feelings of virility and power behind a
loaded gun or the camaraderie which makes dismember-
ing the dead seem noble?*

Enshrouded in a self-erected tomb of guilt and
shame, Larson lay utterly still. He curled into a
fetal position as a stream of tears wound uncontrollable lines around his cheeks. The voices he
heard sounded dulled by distance.

". . .close enough to Forste-Mar. We'll take him
to the dream-reader."

"We'll talk later. Can you do something for him?"

Leaves crunched beside him as Silme approached
and laid her palms gently on his shoulders. Larson raised his head. His tear-blurred vision dis-
torted her beauty to shapelessness. She whispered
seemingly meaningless syllables, and the scattered
shards of Larson's rationality fused together as
her spell blanketed him with peace. As he opened
his mouth to speak, he fell into dreamless bliss.

Larson awoke to a dull mental ache, like an old
scar in cold weather. Sunlight was already slanting
through the branches. He had overslept. He leaped
to his feet and bit off an expletive as Silme rose to
meet him.

"Here." She pushed a fist-sized strip of jerked

venison into his hands. "We'd best be off if we're to reach town by midday."

"Town?" Rubbing his swollen eyes, Larson glanced toward Gaelinar, who was examining the sharpened edge of his katana with approval.

The Kensei pocketed the whetstone and sheathed his sword. "Forste-Mar. It's Silme's hometown." He pointed vaguely northward.

Larson followed the gesture mechanically as he mulled over all the incredible things that had happened to him recently. More accustomed to his new surroundings, now he began to consider details which earlier had been blurred by the necessity for self-preservation. He became aware of the language he spoke as fluently as his companions, a melodious singsong which he supposed was Old Norse. He could not guess why the cold slap of wind did not chill him after the suffocating jungle heat, nor why he remained clean-shaven after two days without a razor.

Larson idly chewed mouthfuls of meat as their journey through the evergreen forest resumed. The clustered trees restricted undergrowth yet remained sparse enough for clear vision and passage. Yearning for a new identity, he paid little attention to their trail. *Al Larson died in Vietnam. Let him keep his memories of atrocity and evil. I am Allerum, an elf without a past on a quest sanctioned by gods.*

Despite the veracity of the sentiment, Larson's conscience resisted. Ugly recollections fought for control, bloody scenes witnessed by the man he had just denounced; but in the sanctity of the forest, Larson held such thoughts in check. His eyes followed Silme, and he surrendered to a thrill of desire. She moved soundlessly, like a woodland being. For all the effort it cost her, the forest might have adapted to suit her rather than she to it.

Gaelinar pushed past Larson and caught the hand in which Silme held her sapphire-tipped staff. The gesture drew Larson from his struggle with self-identity. Until that moment, he'd never considered there might be more to his companions' relationship than mere friendship. The idea drove him to a sadness which flared to fury. He glared as Silme answered Gaelinar's whispered words with a laugh, and the Kensei took the lead of the party.

He must be twice her age, Larson reminded himself in a rage. Yet jealousy did not blind him to an important fact. He had no way to judge Silme's years. Surely a powerful sorceress could warp time's ravishings with illusion. His stomach lurched at the notion. Beauty by magic seemed deceitful. *Yet,* Larson thought as reason dispersed anger, *why should Silme not take advantage of her craft?* Recognition of his own shallowness made Larson flush. There was more to Silme than comeliness. She demonstrated poise, empathy, generosity, pride, and a confidence he sorely missed in himself.

Ruffled by his ponderings, Larson turned his attention back to their surroundings. The terrain grew more hilly, swarming with foxgrape and low, twisted bushes. Passage grew easier as brush gave way to discernible trails beaten to mud by feet, hooves, and wagon wheels. The woods broke suddenly to fields of wind-bowed grain, and the weed-grown path became an obvious road with branches and byways.

Larson hesitated, accustomed to the waist-high, leech-infested swamps of the rice paddies. Gaelinar and Silme continued down the roadway between wheat fields without any apparent worry. But as they turned simultaneously to urge Larson forward, he recognized a solemnity which had escaped him during the journey. He trotted to Silme's side, stared into her eyes, and demanded stridently, "What's the matter?"

She lowered her head until billows of golden hair obscured her face. Her knuckles whitened about her dragonstaff, and she spoke in a dry, quavering whisper. "After your dream I sought Vidarr's guidance. He didn't respond." She raised water-glazed eyes to Larson's curious stare.

A reply seemed necessary, but Larson could think of none. He tried to keep a patronizing tone from his question.

"Does he usually answer you?"

"With images at least." Silme threw back her locks to reveal a face drawn with concern. "I'm his favored attendant. Something terrible has happened."

Unfamiliar with the dealings between gods and men, Larson could offer no real reassurance. He reached for Silme, but Kensei Gaelinar caught his forearm with a tortured cry. "Look there!"

Larson followed the old man's stare. White smoke funneled toward the sky from beyond the next rise. Gaelinar broke into a run, and his companions followed. Larson stubbed a toe in his haste, and his soft, doeskin moccasins did little to dull the impact. Cursing and limping, he caught up with Gaelinar at the hilltop, and the scene below made him forget his pain. Flames danced around an overturned wagon. Beside it, two men pinned a struggling figure to the ground while a third swayed, locked to the wild lurches of the prisoner.

High-pitched, panicked screams drowned Larson's own attempts at breath and cut him to the heart.

Every man draws his limit at an atrocity no amount of coercion could force him to commit. Larson's was rape. More than once, he had turned away while peers in uniform shamed and killed daughters before their helpless fathers. Too moral to join in, at the same time he was unable to risk provoking men on whom his life depended. So he had remained silent, seared by the guilt of a tacit condemnation which might have been approval for all it served the victim or his own conscience. All these thoughts condensed to a boil of emotion.

"Wait!" screamed Silme.

But Gaelinar sprinted down the roadway, howling, "Allerum, charge!" And, hearing his cry, the bandits scrambled for weapons.

After nearly a year of staking his life on strangers' orders, Larson obeyed Gaelinar without thought. He ran within thirty yards of the conflict before he remembered he could not wield his sword. He stopped abruptly as Gaelinar leaped at one of the rapists. Steel chimed as the bandit's sword crashed against the Kensei's shoto. Gaelinar's katana cut a silver arc and cleaved the bandit's neck.

Before Larson could react with even a gasp, one of the bandits closed the gap between them, brandishing a knife in his left hand and a short scimitar in his right. Forced to defend himself, Larson grasped Valvitnir's hilt and pulled. The sword came free with surprising ease and blazed blue as Larson made an awkward lunge. His opponent retreated before the longer weapon.

Larson thrust repeatedly. The bandit redirected the wild strokes with deft flicks of his scimitar. Sweat trickled down Larson's face in a cold stream.

Patience and skill would win this match, and he fell short on both. He hoped Gaelinar would finish his own battle before Larson lost the advantage of distance. Then, he caught sight of the mud-caked figure on the road. *The victim of the bandits' cruel assault was a young boy.*

Anger broke Larson's timing. His opponent dodged under his guard. Steel lanced toward his throat. Sacrificing balance, Larson caught the bandit's left wrist in his hand. The scimitar jarred around his crossguard, and the close range rendered Valvitnir useless. With his right hand locked to his enemy's wrist, Larson scarcely had time to react to the scimitar which flashed for his chest. He dropped his sword. Steel tumbled, and the hilt struck his stubbed toe. Pain shot to his knee. His freed fingers fended off the bandit's other wrist. The scimitar quivered inches from his cheek.

A gasp broke from the bandit with the odor of rotting teeth. He yanked free with a strength which wrenched every tendon in Larson's forearm. The elf responded sluggishly. The scimitar would cut him down before he could regain his grip. Resigned to a second death, he dodged as best he could. Suddenly, steel flashed from the shadows. A hunting blade in the grip of the ravaged child severed the bandit's hamstring, and he reeled backward. Larson's foot lashed into his opponent's groin. The bandit dropped, limp as a rag.

Sweat stung Larson's eyes and splintered the scene to bluish points of light. He dropped to his knees beside the writhing bandit. His hand closed on the hilt of the abandoned scimitar, and he thrust for his enemy's heaving chest. The bandit cringed flat with a strangled whimper, eyes wild with fear. Realization battered Larson like a blow.

He pulled the strike a finger's breadth from the bandit's heart, and the scimitar flopped from his hand like a wounded quail. *The man is helpless. Have I become so callous I kill without thought?*

The bandit's lips set, puzzled. A shadow fell across his drawn face, and light flashed overhead. Larson sprang aside as Gaelinar's katana whisked past him and carved a line of blood across the bandit's throat. The body spasmed in death, its face locked in surprise permanent as a mask.

Larson heard himself scream. His mind tore free from his body, plunging him into an older, more familiar world. Comprehension darkened, than broke in a flash to memory of boot-scuffed dust flickering in the midday heat. It was noon, time for him and Brent Hamill to replace Gavin and Fisher as perimeter guard. Hamill was a newcomer to Aku Nanh, a one week "fucking new guy" who had not yet seen his first fire fight. Though Hamill's inexperience endangered them, Larson liked him and felt obligated to help him through his initiation into Vietnam.

The past few weeks had been unusually quiet which pleased Larson but made many of his companions bored and impatient. Hamill's eyes jumped excitedly as he eyed the wall of sand bags which enclosed the fire base. Larson spared an encouraging smile. As they neared their station, a single shot rang above the general din of conversations. Fisher's good-natured curse was nearly lost beneath Gavin's laughter.

Larson dodged around a grass hut, Hamill close behind. At the perimeter, Gavin hunched over his gun while Fisher baited him like a catcher on a baseball field. Hamill's eyes widened with innocent interest as Larson called to his companions. "What are you doing?"

Gavin glanced over his shoulder and gestured Larson forward. When Hamill and Larson reached the sand bags, Gavin pointed across the tank-cleared plain. A stooped figure waddled along a winding road, barely discernible as an elderly woman. "So?" asked Larson.

"Five bucks to the guy what hits her," explained Fisher with a fiendish smile. "Try your hand?"

Hamill made a pained noise. Larson looked quickly from newcomer to friend, then transformed the shocked movement into a negative toss of his head.

Gavin shrugged and returned to his task. The M-16 spoke once, the woman continued undaunted, and Gavin crawled aside. Fisher moved into position. He spat on his hands, wiped them on his overlarge pants, and hunched over the gun.

Larson avoided Hamill's frantic glances. He knew Gavin and Fisher were merely working off hostility. The woman walked well beyond reasonable target range, and, apparently, she had taken no notice of their potshots.

Hamill grew more distressed. He caught Larson's forearm, and his grip tightened painfully as Gavin and Fisher passed the M-16 twice more between them. When Larson finally turned his attention to Hamill, the newcomer mouthed the words, "Make them stop."

Larson shook him off, not comfortable with the situation, yet unwilling to side with an FNG against friends. Hamill balled his hands together and paced wildly. Crazed beyond understanding, he stopped without warning, swung his M-16 from his shoulder, lined and fired. Soundlessly, the old woman fell to the ground.

Hamill's mouth wrenched open and his face puckered. Larson cringed from the inevitable scream, but Hamill stood silent, like a movie without sound. The gun slid from his hands and thumped to the ground. His dull brown eyes stared through Larson, and he staggered toward the huts as if drunk.

Larson turned to follow, but Fisher caught the back of his shirt. "Shit, Larson. Leave the poor FNG alone. You like some dude hoverin' over you after your first kill?"

Larson paused as Hamill disappeared around a grass hut. "You don't have to be the guy's mother," Gavin added. "Everyone goes through it. You went through it; I went through it. He'll feel like shit with you watching him puke or cry or both. And you ain't going to feel too great either. When . . ."

A pistol shot sounded in the compound, from the general direction of Larson's hut. *Ohmygod!* Larson sprinted toward his quarters with a single coherent thought. *Let it be a rat. Oh, shit, let it be a goddamn rat!* Although trained to his peak physical condition, Larson was out of breath by the time he rounded the corner and burst through the door to his hut. His heart hammered, loud and consistent as machine gun fire. His gaze played over the familiar disarray and settled on the body in his own bunk. Hamill lay still as if in sleep. The .45 automatic lay across his left thigh. His eyes remained open, as if staring at some horrifying sight. Blood spurted from his mangled chin.

"No!" Larson screamed to ears which could not hear. His first aid training surfaced with mechanical efficiency. *For bleeding, apply direct pressure.* Larson covered the ground between himself and Hamill in a single heroic bound. Need usurped thought. Larson locked his hands on the tatters of Hamill's face. Shards of bone and teeth gashed his palms, and his blood mingled freely with the scarlet spring ebbing from his patient.

"Al, stop! There's nothing you can do. He's dead. . . ."

"There's nothing you can do. He's dead." The words were the same, but the voice was from another world. Larson focused on the blood which colored his fingers dull red. The chin cupped between his hands sported two days' growth of beard; the eyes were mercifully closed in death. Larson raised his gaze to the burning wagon. Before it, Gaelinar held the struggling boy. "Child, it's too late. Your uncle is dead."

Dazed, Larson recoiled from the corpse. He whirled to stare at the glowing blue sword, and its brilliance returned him to a reality found only in legend. Slowly, he reached for it. Another object caught his eye, a glass bottle with a hand-lettered label. He retrieved both, jammed the sword into its sheath, and examined the phial. A thick, honey-colored liquid sloshed behind the words: *Crullian's Marvelous Cure.*

Near the dying flames, the boy ceased his furious kicks and punches. He fell against Gaelinar's loose-fitting garb, sobbing. The swordmaster, who had just mercilessly killed three men, held the child in the folds of his robe, face drawn with genuine concern.

Silme strode from behind the wreckage, and her reprimand was singularly tactless. "You may be a sword saint, Kensei. But by Vidarr's shoe, someone's got to teach you to think."

Gaelinar returned her accusation with unbroken confidence. "I'm sorry we got in your way. We couldn't take a chance your spells might hit the boy. Besides," he smiled sheepishly. "I was mad."

The boy pulled away to face Silme. He was small; Larson guessed him to be about ten years old. Raven-hued hair covered his head in a tangle, and his skin was light olive. His quick, blue eyes seemed out of place, and they betrayed some Northern blood mixed with a darker, Eastern race. It was obvious he was some sort of half-breed. Larson followed the boy's gaze from a pair of severely burned legs protruding beneath the charred wagon to Silme. The child clamped hands to his face and announced shrilly, "You're Dragonrank!"

Silme nodded in reply.

The boy's words tumbled over one another, the murdered uncle momentarily forgotten in his excitement. "My great, great grandfather was Dragonrank. And my uncle Crullian knew some magic, too. He's a healer. . . ." He broke off suddenly, and his speech decreased in tempo and volume. "*Was* a healer."

Larson walked over to his companions and stood at Gaelinar's side as Silme quickly changed the subject. "What's your name, child?"

"Brendor," the child introduced himself. "And I'm a wizard, too. Watch!"

Silme made only a half-hearted attempt to stop him. Curious, Larson watched as the child pointed a finger at Gaelinar's face and screamed, "Shave!"

As if in direct defiance of Brendor's command, whiskers sprouted from the Kensei's chin. Gaelinar loosed a startled cry, and Silme hid an amused smile behind her hand. Brendor's face flushed scarlet, and he tried again. "Shave!"

Soft, black hair coated Gaelinar's right cheek.
Despite the fact—Larson's tension had been heightened by the brutal slayings and flashbacks, he
broke into uncontrollable laughter. Gaelinar's eyes
narrowed in annoyance. Brendor seemed drained.
Yet he drew a deep breath, stomped his sandaled
foot in the dirt, and screamed his command in
frustration. "SHAVE!"

Larson's face tingled strangely as hair grew in
random patches. His chuckles died to an incoherent grumble, and he rubbed at the oddly-placed
stubble. Winded and purple-faced, Brendor relin-
quished his spell and dropped his arms. He glanced
at his uncle's smoldering corpse beneath the wagon,
and the sight wrenched a new volley of tears from
his pale eyes.

Gaelinar made a subtle gesture. Silme nodded
slightly, put an arm about the child's shoulders,
and led him down the road toward the town of
Forste-Mar. While Larson watched, woman and
boy disappeared around a bend in the road among
the wheat stalks. Once they passed beyond his
view, Larson turned toward the wagon to find
Gaelinar stoking the waning fire with twigs and
branches. Without question, he joined in the effort, dragging debris from the forest to feed the
flames that were devouring Crullian's body.

The fire flared to brilliance. Gaelinar knelt before it with bowed head and spoke the words of
farewell. "Good-bye from Midgard to the healer
Crullian. May he have died with dignity and the
gods find him worthy of Valhalla or whatever
haven in which he believed."

After Gaelinar's ruthless swordplay, Larson found
the Kensei's compassionate prayer a surprise. *Good
and evil may be more well defined in this world,* he

mused. *But they remain relative.* Absorbed by this
new abstraction, Larson failed to notice as Gaelinar
hauled the three dead bandits within half a yard
of the pyre. The smell of death, grain fields, and
the roaring red flames against a background of
forest formed a familiar knot in Larson's gut.
Caught in the past, he stared until his eyes wa-
tered from pain.

Gaelinar's hand on his wrist rescued Larson from
flashback. He started, acutely aware of every line
on the Kensei's face, from the grim creases in his
forehead to the sweep of his newly-grown beard.
"If you're not going to help, at least hold this for
the boy." Gaelinar tossed a tied linen pouch torn
from a bandit's belt. The cloth muffled the clink
of coins as Larson caught the offering.

"I'll also help." Larson smiled, pocketed the
pouch, and added teasingly, "Since you're too weak
to do it yourself." He hefted one of the bandits by
the armpits. Gaelinar returned the grin and lifted
the corpse by the ankles. In this manner, they
tossed all the rapists' bodies on the pyre without
benefit of epitaph.

The duty of disposing of the corpses dispatched,
the two men started off along the road through
the wheat. At a safe distance from the smoke,
Gaelinar stopped so abruptly his odd, black-
trimmed robes swayed about his hips. Larson
whirled. Gaelinar bowed with a politeness his words
did not match. "You look ridiculous with clumps
of fuzz on your face, hero. Do you have something to take it off with before we rejoin Silme?"

Larson shook his head, grievously aware Freyr
had ill-equipped him for whatever monumental
task recalled him from the future.

"Here then." Gaelinar produced a knife from

the folds of his cloak and tossed it in a gentle arc. He frowned as Larson let the blade fall to the ground at his feet.

Larson hefted the knife uncertainly. Unused to using a dagger as a shaving tool, he waited until Gaelinar drew a second blade and, as hair rasped from the Kensei's chin, tried to imitate his companion's practiced motion. The unsharpened side of the blade settled awkwardly into Larson's hand, pinned to his palm by the tips of his fingers. He set the edge against his cheek and scraped. The knife carved hair and skin from his face with stinging pain. Blood trickled across his fingers, and Larson loosed a violent curse. He granted Gaelinar a glare which dared the man to laugh, but the Kensei kept his thoughts well hidden.

Larson pressed his hand to his cheek until the bleeding slowed. His second, more timid pass with the knife blade went smoother. Gaelinar finished quickly, flicked stubble from his dagger, and waited in silence while Larson struggled with an ineptness which covered his face with nicks. Still, Gaelinar said nothing until Larson finished his task, wiped congealing blood from the steel, and wrapped the dagger in its proffered sheath.

Gaelinar spoke in a voice free of emotion. "Don't be embarrassed. I understand why you can't shave; elves don't have facial hair . . ."

Of course. The revelation made Larson feel foolish. He had forgotten to consider the differences between men and elves. Perhaps his transformation also accounted for his strange tolerance to colder weather. Another thought caused him to break into a sweat which burned the lacerations on his face. *Perhaps elves and humans cannot interbreed—which makes my love for Silme both futile and ludicrous.* The idea so unnerved Larson, he nearly forgot that Gaelinar had not finished his speech.

". . . but I don't know how you've survived this long without sword training," continued the weaponmaster.

Not trusting himself to speak, Larson made a noncommittal gesture.

Gaelinar took the knife from Larson. "I don't mean to insult you, but if you travel with Silme and myself you'll have need of skill. An incompetent swordsman is as dangerous to his companions as to himself. . . ."

Larson nodded dreamily as his thoughts drifted toward Hamill. *An unpredictable hand on a swordhilt, a shaking hand on a gun trigger . . .*

The whipcrack force of Gaelinar's voice returned Larson to awareness. "I'll teach you if you wish. But I warn you, I settle for nothing short of perfection. My lessons will be the most grueling you'll ever endure."

Larson recalled basic training and bit back a skeptical smile. He nodded tacit assent.

Darkness descended upon Larson and his companions while they were still several hours from Forste-Mar. They set up camp in the sparser woodlands near the roadway. Brendor fell asleep immediately, apparently exhausted from the bandits' attack, mental anguish, and his feeble attempts at magic. Gaelinar crouched with his back against a tree, his gaze locked on Silme as she murmured the incantations which formed her wards. Larson stretched out beside the Kensei, his fingers locked beneath his head as a pillow while he stared at the stars through the interlaced branches.

Larson yawned. *It took me six weeks of boot camp to*

*learn the rules of war and six months of combat to
realize war has no rules. Now, in three days, I've come
to accept elves and swords as commonplace.* He rolled
to his side and watched Silme pause as the enchantments of her wards faded into the gloom of
night. *And then, there is magic.* The memory of
Bramin's cruelties in the woodlands made Larson
break into a cold sweat. *If laws govern or moderate its
use, they are lenient. For all my knowledge of future
technology, I cannot stand against Bramin.*

Larson fidgeted, bothered by these new ideas. *I
thought the Norse gods aided their warriors in battle, not
abandoned them without knowledge of purpose in a
world of undefeatable enemies. I've risked my life too
long for causes I don't understand. Bramin wants my
sword, not me. And Silme and Gaelinar seem far more
qualified to protect it.* His hand fell to the buckle of
his sword belt.

A foreign sense of urgency swept through Larson. Freyr's authoritative voice seemed to echo in
his mind. "Stop, please. It is true gods meddle in
the lives of men, but you have entered the affairs
of gods. I am helpless to protect you."

Stunned by Freyr's unexpected appearance, Larson said nothing.

Freyr continued. "The gods have vowed not to
work against one another or the Fates. To you it
may seem ridiculous, but without such laws nothing could ever get done. For every deity who
wishes to stir up war, another would cultivate peace.
Every action, every creation would have an antagonist. Soon, we would generate the chaos we guard
against; the gods would war against one another
in a combat which would not end until it encompassed the nine worlds.

Larson's mind responded sluggishly. "But why me?" he whispered.

Freyr hesitated. "I've seen your world. I brought you from a place where women, children, dirt, and trees were as dangerous as any sword. You learned to fear the few things in life a man should be able to trust. Love lost its allure before the constant threat of death which claimed friends, lovers, and enemies indiscriminately. Nothing remained permanent. In moments, rivers dried and forests exploded to barren plains. Amid colored lights and noise, the ground quaked with enough force to uproot the World Tree, and countless lives were spilled with every shrill of the war god's laughter. Like Valhalla's Einherjar, soldiers fought brave battles by day, but the dead never rose and the living lost sleep guarding against the dragons which stalked the jungles. Who is better qualified to prevent Ragnarok than a man who suffered its equal?"

Larson bit his lip, focusing on Freyr's words rather than the concepts they represented and the memories they inspired. He whispered a question. "Ragnarok? The war fated to destroy all but a handful of gods and men. Is it my mission to prevent such a thing?"

Freyr's presence in Larson's mind went pensive. "I'm . . . not certain. I can tell you nothing more. Already I have revealed more than my vows allow. I must never contact you again. If Loki's chaos can be halted, another god shall make your quest clear. If not, my efforts have only thrown you into a war as twisted as the one which killed you. But this one can claim your soul as well as your life. Forgive me." As suddenly as it had come, Freyr's manifestation disappeared.

Sweat beaded Larson's brow. "Freyr. Freyr!"

Larson received no answer, but Silme and Gaelinar stared. "J-just a prayer." Larson defended himself lamely. He curled into a fetal position on the grass. Despite his muddled thought, Freyr's disquieting revelations, and his companions' suspicions, he fell into a wary slumber.

The subtle breaking of brush startled Larson awake. His heart pounded. He forced himself to inhale and exhale slowly, counting each breath until the rhythm lulled him to an inner calmness. His senses focused on the irregular, soft sounds of movement through the brush. Gradually, he worked his hand to his side where his gun should sit. His fingers brushed empty ground. Suppressing a curse, he explored the clearing around him. The side of his hand met the hilt of his sword; and, for a time, he lay confused.

A hand pressed his shoulder reassuringly, and Gaelinar's familiar voice hissed into his ear. "Be still. Just watch."

Curiosity replaced Larson's bewilderment. His palm curled around Valvitnir's hilt. His gaze swept the brush at the edge of camp where a hunched, dark figure slithered into view and paused momentarily. Larson's grip tightened. Gaelinar's hand remained on his arm, restraining. Through the slight haze, Larson assessed the man who stalked them. He wore a dark gray tunic. Moonlight emphasized the pallor of his hair and beard. He crawled with calculated caution.

The stranger's hand rose, the gesture arrested as suddenly as if he'd struck a wall. White-hot flames burst around his fingers. He screamed, reeling back as Silme's wards sprang to view in an intertwining pattern around the camp. Gaeliner and Larson leaped to their feet simultaneously as the stranger sprinted into the woods, howling in pain.

A distant voice yelled, "Gilbyr!" Nearby, a curse sounded above the panicked screams. "Damn the dark elf! He never mentioned magic. Gilbyr!" Arrows arched through the air.

"Incoming!" Instinctively, Larson dove to the ground. The arrows struck the magical barrier and, unable to pass through it, plummeted to earth in flames. Brush rattled loudly for a short time, and the woods returned to silence.

Brendor spoke in a frightened whine, and his question mirrored Larson's thoughts. "What happened?"

Silme hadn't even stirred during the attack. Her reply seemed inappropriately calm. "A few of Bramin's lackeys tried to pass my wards. Fools."

Gaelinar resumed his crouch against the tree. Larson remained still, his gaze locked on the forest. "What is 'Gilbyr'?"

Gaelinar closed his eyes. "A name, Allerum. Apparently this Gilbyr has chosen to become our enemy. Therefore, I suggest you remember him."

Larson stared at the glowing waves of Silme's wards, quite certain he could never forget.

CHAPTER 3

Kinslayer

"Every man's sword shall be against his brother."

—Ezekiel 38:21

Brendor whined fretfully as he followed Silme, Gaelinar, and Larson along the road to Forste-Mar. "You promised I could stay till you taught me to do my shave spell right."

"You can't come with us." Silme rubbed at her eyes with an annoyance which made it obvious she had answered his challenge more than once, and she was weakening. "Gaelinar's right. Our task is too dangerous for a child." In a sudden flash of inspiration she added, "You can stay with my mother. She raised two children to Dragonrank."

Larson moved to the roadside as a rickety wagon rolled past, drawn by a gaunt workhorse. Steam issued from the beast's wide nostrils, and the creak of wheels drowned out Brendor's reply. The driver raised his whip in salute. "Heyo, Silme! What brings you home?"

Silme returned the greeting, but the cart lurched past before she could answer the farmer's query.

As the wagon jounced toward the forest, its wheels left no mark on the frozen soil. At the border of Forste-Mar's town square, Larson and his companions left the wheat fields behind for sagging paddocks of lean-fleshed goats.

"You promised." Brendor's face reflected a pleading, childish innocence which Larson could never resist. It reminded him of the doe-eyed entreaties of Ti Sun, a Vietnamese boy who had always managed to relieve him of his rare chocolate bar until . . . Larson's body snapped taut as he tried to force the thought from memory. Imagined gunfire deafened him momentarily, but Silme's soft reply to the child checked Larson's wandering consciousness.

"I only said I'd try. Not everyone can learn magic. You're fortunate to possess even the ability to cast a shave spell wrong. Only a handful of people in the entire realm control as much spell energy as you can now." Silme paused, obviously trying to twist her explanation to her favor. "If you are destined for power the dragonmark will appear. Until then, you'll be happier in town. The wandering life is insecure and often unpleasant. A child—"

Irritated by his mind's erratic lapses into memory, Larson interrupted with a tongue thick and furred as that of a man awakening from a drinking binge. "He knows more about traveling than we do for chrissakes! His uncle was a goddamn snake oil salesman." Suddenly Brendor found an ally.

Until that moment, neither Gaelinar, Silme, nor Brendor had paid Larson much heed. Now they whirled to face him simultaneously. The Kensei cleared his throat. "His uncle was a what?"

"A healer." Larson adopted the native term. "A *traveling* healer." He put a protective arm about Brendor's shoulders, and the boy's mouth twitched into a contented smile. "I'll bet he's never had a home."

"Just Crullian's wagon," Brendor answered on cue.

Silme tossed her head and continued walking into the town proper. "Come on."

Though the argument remained unsettled, Larson knew it had turned in Brendor's favor. He and the boy exchanged furtive smiles as they followed the sorceress in silence. Brendor's round face and partially concealed grin reminded Larson of his younger brother, Timmy, when they had once conspired to dye their sister's underwear green. This familiarity in a world of dragons and berserk wizards soothed, and Larson clung to the normalcy Brendor added to their party.

As they walked, Gaelinar gave Larson a few "we will talk later" looks, then drew up beside the elf. "Silme has business in town, and I think it best I accompany her. You can handle buying mounts and rations." No doubt entered Gaelinar's steady voice despite Larson's numerous previous displays of incompetence.

Grateful for the Kensei's confidence, Larson determined at least to purchase supplies without error. He accepted the pouch of coins Silme offered and listened attentively as she described the lay of the town. "Kortr the horse trader lives on the south side of the main track. You can get a decent horse for five silver, four if you bargain well."

Larson examined the sod-chinked log dwellings ahead which were criss-crossed by hard-packed thoroughfares. Five golden-haired girls passed in a giggling huddle. When they noticed Larson, their laughter ceased abruptly. Quickening their pace, they marked Larson's progress with nervous glances. Puzzled, he watched the retreating figures and considered their strange reactions.

Silme stopped on a large throughway, and her companions surrounded her as she continued. "Hlathum the food seller lives in the cottage beside Kortr. Tell him you want two weeks' traveling rations for three—" She corrected herself. "—four and mention my name. He won't cheat you. As for the innkeeper, Ura always acts like someone pissed in his ale. Don't let him charge you more than a silver for our suite. And . . ."

"Silme!" Gaelinar interrupted in a tone sharp as his katana. "The elf and the boy are perfectly capable of walking, talking, and breathing without your expert advice. Let's go."

As Silme and Gaelinar started down a side street, the sorceress added over her shoulder, "Get some dinner at the inn. We'll meet you there tonight."

Recalling the fear he'd inspired in the passing girls, Larson failed to acknowledge Silme's farewell. Without his more experienced companions for the first time in days, doubts rushed down upon him. The girls' reaction reminded him that he inhabited an elf's body, and Gaelinar's explanation when they were still in the distant woods seemed acutely important now: *Mostly, the sidelong glances and whispered comments which follow any stranger viewed as different will accompany you throughout the world of Midgard.* Larson wondered how he would fare in the town where Bramin was raised.

Unaccustomed to the horse-and-cart traffic of Forste-Mar, Larson found road crossings almost unbearable. Invariably, he waited long minutes while slower vehicles dawdled down the byways or earned vicious epithets when he tried to dodge before more swiftly moving carts. Twice, Brendor pulled him away from the steel-shod hooves of galloping mares. After that, Larson let the boy set their pace and wondered idly whether he could readjust to cars and trucks if he ever returned to the States.

Despite the overlong and often hostile gazes the populace accorded Larson, his marketing went smoothly. After he mentioned Silme's name, his session with Hlathum became brief and painless. The foodstuffs lay wrapped in portions in a large sack which Larson slung across his back. As if to conclude business as swiftly as possible, the horse merchant requested only seventeen silver for the four mounts Larson later stabled at the inn. Self-content and hungry, the elf ushered Brendor into the dimly-lit interior of Ura's Inn and selected a table in the farthest corner.

The round-topped table was pine, beer-stained and pushed tight against the chamber wall. Larson caught an outer edge and inched it forward. He maneuvered a chair into the vacant corner and sat. Back pressed to the wall, he surveyed the barroom and its patrons sitting at tables arranged in three neat rows of three. Each table bore a single candle which chased darkness in a broad semicircle, enhancing shadows on the ceiling. Raw-boned, blond-haired humans conversed in couples or groups of four or five. A man proportioned like a middle linebacker stood alone at the bar. A pewter mug rested near his elbow, but the huge stranger seemed more interested in Larson than in his drink. While Larson met the man's stare with forced nonchalance, Brendor took a seat at his left.

A boy scarcely older than the healer's nephew strode around the tables and positioned himself between Larson and Brendor. He shifted from foot to foot uncomfortably. "Can I get you something?"

Larson replied without thought. *"Bami-bam, boy-san."*

Brendor started. The sudden movement drew Larson's attention from the man at the bar. "Excuse me, sir?" asked the serving boy nervously.

"Um . . ." stammered Larson. Lulled by the familiar surroundings of a tavern, he suddenly realized he had ordered in Vietnamese. "W-what do you suggest?"

The boy knotted his hands on the tabletop, obviously unsettled by his customer. "Special today is lamb breast, fresh bread, and cheese with ale."

"Fine." Larson slanted a friendly glance at Brendor. "Sound good?"

Coins clicked as Brendor closed a hand over the pouch of silver Gaelinar had rescued from the bandits. "I'll have the same."

The boy nodded and trotted behind the bar to relay the order. Larson returned his attention to the tavern's interior. Struck by the smokeless clarity of the candle light, he would have paid all the money remaining in Silme's pouch for a pack of cigarettes or a single joint. A gesture in Larson's direction swung his gaze to the exit where a man in ragged homespun downed his drink in a single gulp, abandoned his two companions, and ducked out the door. The man's two friends avoided Larson's stare.

Though troubled by the surreptitious exchange, Larson persuaded himself his mistrust stemmed from war-inspired paranoia. *Why should peasants in a town at peace wish to harm a stranger, even if he is an outsider?* The self-questioning revived recent memory. When Larson had first arrived in this unusual world, Bramin had attacked furiously without provocation. Torn between common sense and experience, Larson considered running from the inn. The serving boy approached with a plateful of food. Ultimately, its mouthwatering aroma convinced Larson to stay.

The boy set the wooden dishes before his patrons and scuttled back to the bar. Larson's first few mouthfuls took the edge from his hunger and with it his appreciation for the meal. He reached for a nonexistent salt shaker, caught himself, and leaned back with a sigh. "Everything in this world tastes the same. Isn't there any salt?"

Brendor dropped a lamb rib from fingers slick with grease. "Salt? I can do that!" Before Larson thought to protest, the boy performed a graceless gesture and spoke in a high-pitched whisper. "Salt!"

Nothing obvious happened, although Brendor panted with exertion. Relieved, Larson stroked the crusted scabs on his cheeks, a memento of Brendor's last magical endeavor. Painfully aware of his own inadequacies, Larson flashed the boy an understanding smile. Dwelling on the matter might embarrass Brendor, and so the elf passed it off with casual indulgence. "Tough luck, kid." He took a bite of cheese. A flavor bitter as poison spread through his mouth and pinched his face until he gagged. Between coughs which expelled half-chewed morsels, Larson managed to speak. "I asked for ... salt ... not soap!" He washed the taste from his mouth with a gulp of ale, left with watering eyes, a sore throat, and a memory that made his nose wrinkle with disgust.

Appetite ruined, Larson avoided Brendor's shamefully lowered face. He pushed his chair from the table and walked to the bar where a fat inn-keeper flicked at the warped pine counter with a damp rag. Ura seemed to take no notice of the approaching elf, but the huge man at the bar squared his shoulders and edged closer. The move-ment put Larson on the defensive, but he forced aside discomfort as he prepared to bargain with the barkeep. "I'd like to rent a suite," he said in a businesslike voice which revealed none of his trep-idations. Familiar with streetside markets, Larson prepared to snap back half the quoted price.

Ura raised his head. "Fourteen silver."

"S-what?" Composure lost, Larson stared. Ura's rate was too far beyond expectation to be other than a mistake.

"Fourteen silver," repeated Ura. He regarded Larson with scornful disinterest.

"That's outrageous!"

Ura shrugged. "Fourteen silver," he said with indisputable finality. "Take it or get out of my inn."

Larson opened his mouth to protest, but an-other man spoke from the tavern doorway. "You heard him. This place smells bad enough without your kind, elf!"

Larson caught at one pointed ear, suddenly feel-ing like an American in a North Vietnamese prison camp. He turned to his antagonist with feigned unconcern and adopted a false smile. The man at the door stood several inches taller than him, and Larson did not care to discover how much of the bulk beneath his chain shirt was padding. Likely the stranger was a member of Forste-Mar's guard force, summoned by the man who had left the bar earlier and now stood near the guardsman.

Brendor came to Larson's side. Afraid for the child's life, Larson stepped before him protectively. To his relief, a stranger at one of the tables came to their defense. "He's not going to hurt anyone, Anrad. He's a *light* elf."

Larson bit his lip with understanding. Again Gaelinar's description returned to him, and nervous energy revived the most distressing sentence of his explanation: *At times, dark elves are welcomed because of the legends of light elves, and light elves are slain for the ancient crimes of their dark cousins.* Bramin had turned the town of Forste-Mar against faery folk, but a Dragonrank mage was too powerful for peasants' vengeance. Over years, unvented hatred had intensified, seeking a victim. Unless Larson acted with heroic discretion, he might pay with his and Brendor's lives for Bramin's evil. He faced the barkeep again. "I just want . . ."

"Fourteen silver and not one copper less," said Ura with pointed hostility.

Goaded by Ura's patrons, Anrad stepped boldly into the barroom's center. "Let him sleep in the stables for two silver."

Steeling himself, Larson turned. His fingers plucked nervously at his tunic, but his words were carefully selected and innocuously spoken. "It only cost a copper for the horses."

Anrad folded his arms across his broad chest. "But you'll want to bed every beast in the stable." His gaze dropped to Brendor, and his lips twisted in a sneer. "Oh, but I see you've brought your own entertainment."

Brendor pushed in front of Larson. Red-faced with the perfect rage only a child can experience, he struggled to speak without screaming. "Your mother's safe, there are no asses in the stable!"

Anrad's face flushed. He raised a hand threateningly. "You little bastard."

Anger flared in Larson. Suddenly beyond thought of the consequences, he cocked his fist and leaped for the guardsman. A callused palm caught Larson's wrist. He was wrenched forcefully about to face the huge man at the bar whose bear-sized hand locked on his arm. "You two want to kill each other, do it outside!"

"Fine!" Anrad marched out the door, chuckling, and the crowd of patrons funneled into the street.

No stranger to bar fights, Larson tore free of the bouncer's grip and strode toward the door. Memory of his reflection in the pond bred doubts. This elf-form robbed him of the bulk won from years of wrestling and weight training. He could only hope he had retained some of his strength, and he would have to remember to throw full effort into every punch. Intent on strategy, Larson strode blindly from the inn and nearly impaled himself on Anrad's naked sword.

Larson recoiled with a yell. His fist closed on Valvitnir's hilt, and the blade sprang from its sheath so quickly he was unsure whether he or the sword initiated the movement. Anrad swept for Larson's chest. Larson ducked behind Valvitnir. Sword crashed against sword, and Anrad's blade shattered to faintly glowing shards.

Anrad retreated, eyes wild. More familiar with fist fighting, Larson handed his sword to Brendor. "I can take him without a weapon." Hands for-

ward, he closed, prepared to pummel the guardsman before he could recover from surprise. Anrad
dropped his useless hilt and dodged under Larson's swing. His return punch crashed against the
elf's jaw, hurling him backward. Larson tried to
block, but the guard's other fist thudded into his
gut, stealing breath.

Larson staggered. The cries of the crowd blended
to undecipherable noise. Anrad's pale fist rushed
toward his face. Larson blocked with his left arm,
then cut downward and caught the guardsman's
wrist. He seized Anrad's elbow in his right hand
and whipped his opponent around in a wrestling
drag. Larson's arm closed about Anrad's neck.
The guard struggled momentarily then dropped
to the ground, breathless.

Pain-maddened, Larson kicked Anrad's mailed
side. Impact with the heavy chain links shot agony
along Larson's foot. Anrad winced with a gasp.
Larson smashed his heel into Anrad's face. Bones
cracked, and blood poured from the guardsman's
nose. Anrad lay with closed eyes, emitting small
panting sobs.

Only then did Larson consider the battle won.
In the same situation, James Bond or Errol Flynn
would have delivered some witty line and strode
off into the sunset. But Larson felt too disgusted
for endearing dramatization. His jaw ached with
every heartbeat, and he could taste blood. Without a word, he wheeled away.

Dust billowed around the scene of the fight.
Larson waited until it settled and searched for
Brendor. The boy was gone. Larson's wits scattered as panic replaced ire. He cast about frantically. "Brendor. Where's my sword? Brendor?"

Larson received no reply from anywhere in the

crowd. He spun awkwardly, like a drunken dancer, without sighting the boy. Brendor and Valvitnir had disappeared completely. Larson seized an old man by the collar and jacked him against the tavern wall. "Which way did he go?"

The man pointed a shaking finger toward a narrow throughway between buildings. Dropping his informant, Larson charged through the gaping onlookers. He hurtled down the alleyway, well aware there could be only one enemy. Bramin's use of a child seemed a ruse so obvious he wondered how he had come to overlook it. Booby-trapping children was a favorite trick of the Viet Cong; he should have expected no less from Bramin. Brendor was certainly Bramin's accomplice, placed in a piteous position where Larson and his companions would happen upon him. Once Brendor gained Larson's trust, he waited for an opening to steal the sword. And Larson had fallen for the plan like an idiot, his only comfort the fact that Silme and Gaelinar had been duped as easily as himself.

The roadway forked suddenly. Larson chose his direction at random. Wind blew a discarded rag under his feet, and Larson skirted it instinctively. The pathway narrowed between cottages and ended at a staunch wooden gate. Beyond lay a plowed field. Across acres of sprouting grain stood a cottage. As Larson watched, a small figure darted toward it.

Larson sprang for the gate. A poorly-timed memory slammed his consciousness with a force akin to Anrad's blows. He flinched back as the scene in his head exploded in red light. "They've wired the gate!" screamed Gavin. Even as Larson surrendered to flashback, he pitched himself over the barrier.

The illusion mushroomed to a cloud of fire, and impact with the ground jarred Larson back to the wheat field. Sweat stung his eyes. Field dirt clung to his limbs. He ripped his tunic as he struggled to his feet and sprinted toward the cottage. The child grew more visible as he approached, dark-haired, dressed in tan and blue, and pressed to the mud-chinked stone wall. It was unmistakably Brendor. The boy turned as Larson closed, and his face went pale.

"You conniving little bastard," Larson panted as he seized Brendor's forearm. "I ought to break your goddamned neck."

Brendor's face screwed into a harried mass of wrinkles. "Stop, shhh . . ." He pulled against Larson's grip.

Larson tightened his fist as Brendor fought against him. "Don't 'shhh' me, you little brat. I'll . . ."

Brendor took a sharp intake of breath. His gaze suddenly focused beyond Larson. Menaced from behind, the elf loosed the child. Brendor fell against the wall with a pained whimper. Larson whirled to face two men with drawn swords. A third stood between them, unarmed but no less formidable. A heavy cloth bandage enclosed his right hand. "If you were trying to be subtle," said one, "you failed miserably."

The second man stepped forward. "If you've come for your sword, I may decide to give it to you." Spit sprayed from his mouth as he pronounced each word with gloating force. "Jammed through your ugly, elven heart."

"What do we do with them?" asked the unarmed man.

"Take them inside," replied the first. "I think Bramin would be grateful if we accidentally killed them." He gestured. "Gilbyr, you lead. Then the boy, followed by the elf." His eyes met Larson's. "Do anything we don't like and you earn two swords between your ribs."

The name Gilbyr blazed in Larson's awareness from the previous night when Bramin's bandits tried to break through Silme's wards. He stared at Gilbyr's bandaged hand, recalling the power of the sorceress' white-hot magics. *I can't face Bramin without Silme*. Rising fear blurred memory into purpose. Still uncertain of Brendor's role in the swordnapping, Larson glanced at the boy.

The fear and betrayal stamped across Brendor's features hurt Larson worse than the bandits' gibes and death threats. "They grabbed the sword from me and ran. I tried . . ."

"Silence!" Gilbyr raised his injured hand to strike Brendor and immediately realized his mistake. The thief bit back a scream. Fresh blood colored his bandage. "Another thing you'll pay for. Come along."

Hesitantly, Brendor went to Gilbyr, rubbing elbows skinned from Larson's unceremonious push against the cottage. Bereft of alternatives, Larson followed. He wished he had a means to judge the sword skill of the man behind him.

In a line, captors and victims passed around the cottage. Gilbyr paused before the front door and tripped the latch. Larson fretted, the thought of dying indoors no more palatable than that of dying outside. *Now or never*. The oaken door swung open. As Gilbyr started through the portal, Larson pretended to stumble. The swordsmen lurched with him. Larson shoved Brendor into Gilbyr with

all the strength he could muster. Man and boy
tumbled into the cottage, a twisting wheel of arms
and legs. A blade licked Larson's back as he sprang
through the opening and pulled the door shut
behind him.

Swords thumped against the wood, mingled with
muffled curses. While Gilbyr and Brendor untan-
gled themselves, Larson shot the bolt home, aware
the swordsmen could not quickly break through
solid oak. Fists clenched, Larson turned to engage
Gilbyr. As Brendor freed himself, he stomped on
Gilbyr's wounded hand. Howling curses, Gilbyr
backed toward an open doorway several feet away.
Brendor ran to Larson's side.

Larson advanced. Behind him, the door rattled
beneath the swordsmen's blows. A plan took form,
and he repressed an amused smile which might
ruin its effect. He let his fists go lax and trained
his eyes on Gilbyr. "Stop, fool!" Larson borrowed
the voice of a summoned god from a cheap horror flick.

Gilbyr hesitated.

Larson loosed a rumbling laugh and wished he
sounded less nervous and more evil. "You chose
the wrong victims for your childish prank." He
snapped a hand in Brendor's direction. "This is
no boy, but a master Dragonrank in child form."

Brendor looked as startled as the thief. The
door shuddered and groaned warningly.

Larson sacrificed a dramatic pause for brevity.
"You've already sampled his power. Look at your
hand. He could slay you with a single word, but
your transgressions have gone beyond merciful
death. Now he shall twist your very soul." He
raised his arms for effect and took a threatening
forward step. "Your person will transform to a

wolf-being which feasts upon blood and howls at the full moon. *Men will hunt you down!*"

Wood splintered as a sword tip cracked the door and retreated. Larson kicked Brendor's shin. "Shave, kid," he whispered.

"Shave!" hollered Brendor.

Hair sprang from Gilbyr's face. The thief loosed a blood-curdling shriek and bolted through the crumbling door. The oak panel broke open. Gilbyr spitted himself on his companions' swords, and his screams transformed from panicked to agonized.

Brendor grabbed Larson's arm. "Come on!"

Larson needed no urging. Elf and boy sprang through the rearward portal and found themselves in a small storage room. Behind, Gilbyr's sharp screams rose over the exchanges of the thieves. Brendor clawed at a square of fur which covered the window, but a faintly-glowing sack in the storeroom corner arrested Larson's escape. "The sword!" He crossed the room in two leaping strides and ripped the cloth bag, spilling woolen garments to the bare stone floor.

Dropping to a crouch, Larson buried his hands in the cloth and was rewarded by a touch of metal. His wild gesture flung tunics through the storeroom and uncovered Valvitnir's jeweled hilt. With a relieved sigh, Larson caught the grip as Gilbyr's shrieks subsided to anguished moans in the other room.

Valvitnir quivered in greeting. Its presence inspired a strange joy, lulling Larson's mind to an inner peace instantly shattered by a string of curses from the adjoining room. No sign remained of Brendor but a rumpled pile of furs beneath the window. Larson flung the sword. It flew, straight as an archer's arrow, through the window into the gathering grayness of evening. He scuttled after it.

The rough-hewn stone of the window scraped Larson's skin despite his clothing. He caught the outer ledge, swung his legs between his hands, and hit the ground prepared to run. A short distance ahead, Brendor's slight form darted toward the town square. Closer, Valvitnir flared blue as a beacon.

Instinctively, Larson dropped to the ground, held himself flat and silent in the gloom. Then, remembering that the thieves in this world carried no guns or grenades, he caught the sword hilt and sprinted after the retreating child. Though encumbered by the weapon's weight, Larson overtook Brendor halfway across the plowed field, and matched the child's pace. Like hunted deer, elf and boy bounded across the tract. By the time they reached the gate, Larson's legs ached from the effort, and he had twisted his ankles countless times.

Only when they reached the alley did they dare to look behind. The cottage stood shrouded in haze, but it seemed no thieves dared pursue the elven swordsman and his "master Dragonrank." Larson tried not to imagine who would have suffered Gilbyr's wrath had the thief realized the magic-using adept could be better called inept.

As he regained his breath, Larson looked at Brendor, and the boy returned his stare. "You spoiled my ambush," Brendor accused.

"It's only fair," Larson snapped back. "You ruined my dinner."

Brendor smothered a giggle. "Ruined Gilbyr's face, too."

Struck by the absurdity of the comment after their harrowing series of experiences, Larson laughed so hard he needed to catch the gate to keep his balance. Brendor lapsed into convulsive titterings. Their chortles melded to a gleeful duet as tension broke in a rush of camaraderie. Elf and boy regained composure simultaneously. Then Brendor hiccuped, and they burst into wild laughter again.

Less than a yard deeper in the alley, someone spoke. "Where have you two been?"

Startled, Larson inhaled a mouthful of saliva. No longer laughing, he wheeled to face a thin man in black-trimmed gold robes. The adrenalin rush inspired by Gaelinar's swift, silent appearance strained Larson's cry of welcome.

Gaelinar took no notice. "I thought you'd meet us in the tavern."

"We went exploring." Larson lied, not wishing to explain to the swordmaster how he had disarmed himself in battle and was forced to retrieve his sword from bandits.

Gaelinar fondled the brocade at his sword hilt. "Looking for trouble would better describe it if I'm to believe Ura. He told me you challenged the guard captain."

"Well . . ." started Larson, with no idea how he would finish the sentence.

Gaelinar did not need explanations. He scrutinized Larson in the waning light. "Did you at least win?"

"Of course," Larson said with a false confidence. Impossible as it seemed, his reply was true.

"Good." The Kensei turned in a swirl of gold robes and started down the alley. "Then you should do well with your first sword lesson tonight."

Brendor and Larson trotted behind Gaelinar. "Tonight?" repeated Larson incredulously, feeling very tired.

"Tonight," Gaelinar confirmed with a toss of his gray locks. "But just until dark. I would have started sooner had I known you made a habit of antagonizing guards."

Larson wanted to protest but could think of nothing convincing to say. The alleyway broadened and met the road before Ura's Inn, conspicuously devoid of the afternoon crowd. Forste-Mar had literally closed for the evening.

Gaelinar continued. "Silme settled your tab at the tavern. I've never traveled on Alfheim, Allerum, but here we pay for our meals before we leave the table." He nodded toward the hulking shape of the inn. "Brendor, get some sleep. Silme rented a suite for an infinitely reasonable price, and Ura gave her the sack of rations you left in the barroom. She can get very convincing." The slight smile which played across Gaelinar's lips as he thumbed his sword guard caused Larson to wonder about the Kensei's role in Ura's persuasion.

Brendor headed for the inn, and Gaelinar called after him. "And don't bother Silme until morning!" Swiftly, the Kensei turned and strode along the hard-packed road. "How much do you know about swordplay?"

Larson jogged to keep up with his companion. "Nothing. Believe it or not, men in my world haven't used swords for centuries."

Gaelinar made a disgruntled noise. "I commend the peacefulness of your people. But just because you've put an end to warfare doesn't mean you should forget weapons skills."

"Wha-huh?" Larson's incoherent reply was startled from him. Throughout the last few days, nightmare visions of Vietnam had haunted his waking moments as well as his dreams. Though he would have preferred to erase the war from memory, its actuality was too vivid to deny, even to a friend from a happier world. "I'm afraid my people abandoned swords for more lethal weapons. So long as a world contains men and issues, war will result."

"True enough." Gaelinar ducked beneath an age-blackened rope which enclosed a square of freshly-raked sand. "But disagreement needn't end in death. Many worthy opponents have become allies. And there is a glory to dying in a battle you and an able enemy chose to fight. Men here believe death in valorous combat earns a place in Odin's Valhalla for oneself or a noble foe. There souls battle through the day; those slain rise again each evening in preparation for the final war against Loki and his minions. The infirm and cowardly join Loki's Hel hordes, forced to side against mankind for the cause of utter Chaos."

Larson supposed the roped off area was a practice ground for guards. He followed Gaelinar, convinced the most important phrase in the Kensei's rhetoric was "chose to fight." Vietnam seemed nothing better than a lame excuse to satisfy the cruel fantasies of men and goad eighteen-year-old children to murder and misguided vengeance.

"Philosophy will not save you from my lesson." Gaelinar's katana sprang silently from its sheath. Its tip pointed toward Valvitnir's scabbard. "You will now begin the way."

Larson waited for an explanation which never came. He watched in silence as Gaelinar walked to the center of the field. Faster than Larson could

follow, the Kensei drew his shoto and executed a
strike with its handle. The katana followed with
an upward cut. Gaelinar recovered, both swords
close to his body.

Awed, Larson rested his hand on Valvitnir's
pommel as he watched Gaelinar's swords flow
around the Kensei, scattering reflections of the
rising moon. Then a subtle change in timing gave
his strokes the cruel snap of flames leaping through
kindling. Abruptly, the Kensei stopped. He wiped
sweat from his eyes with the back of his sleeve and
beckoned Larson forward. Expectantly, Larson approached his teacher.

"You must learn much in a short time," said
Gaelinar. "I will teach you a lot, but you will teach
yourself more. Draw your sword."

Larson found Valvitnir's hilt and unsheathed
the sword. The leather molded to his hand, but
the grip shifted like a living thing against his palm
until his thumb, forefinger, and middle finger
rested only lightly on it while his remaining two
fingers held the sword firmly. With a surprised
gasp, Larson let the weapon drop from his hand.
The blade struck the sand with a thump and lay
still.

At Gaelinar's curious look, Larson reclaimed the
sword sheepishly, certain fatigue accounted for
his strange perception. The hilt settled in his grip.
With the patience of wind whittling a mountain
range, Valvitnir again adjusted to the proper position in Larson's hand.

"Good." The Kensei nodded his approval. "I
see you've had some training. You do hold the
sword properly. Now you'll learn your first form.
Watch." Gaelinar sheathed his companion sword
and gripped his katana in his right hand. Larson

watched intently as his teacher positioned himself, left foot ahead and sword low. Gaelinar stepped forward and arched his sword over his head, then drove downward and slightly past his leg.

Larson chuckled inwardly as Gaelinar repeated the maneuver half a dozen times to either side of his body. *This will be easy*, he told himself. Strange laughter accompanied his assessment. Larson spun and saw no one. He and the Kensei were alone, and his teacher was not amused. Confused, Larson dismissed the incident as hallucination, attributing his odd perceptions to fatigue.

Gaelinar returned, grim-faced, and sheathed his katana. "If you know this form within three weeks, I will be pleased."

Shocked, Larson stared. "Three weeks? I can walk and chew gum at the same time."

"Gum?" repeated Gaelinar. He shrugged the strange word off as unimportant.

Evening breezes cut through Larson's ragged tunic, and he shivered. Gaelinar freed his katana and rested its tip on the sand. "Hero, you are a fledgling. At first, an eagle flaps its wings awkwardly and achieves nothing. Eventually, it understands. You are an eaglet without the luxury of time. You must soar and hunt before learning to fly. You will know this kata as nothing you have known before. Guide your sword with your spirit as well as your arm. When you find the way, it will become a part of you. Begin."

Larson shifted from foot to foot, seeking a comfortable stance. He lowered the sword, mimicking Gaelinar, and made a cut toward and past his right leg. Valvitnir jerked back, as if of its own volition. Larson froze. Slowly, he turned an accusatory glance toward Gaelinar who stood patiently waiting for Larson to finish. Puzzled, the elf repeated the attempt, and again the sword pulled to the same position. He gripped the hilt tighter and tried again. Though he struggled against it, the sword still adjusted.

"Allerum!" the Kensei instructed. "You needn't crush your sword. It is not your enemy. Relax. You must control your strokes. Don't swing past and return your blade. Stop the cut nearer your leg. Now, continue."

Valvitnir gleamed red-blue in the last dying rays of the sun. Larson recommenced. Apparently, whatever the sword did was correct. *There are too many odd things in this world to question. Is a sentient sword less likely than dragons or magic?* Its abilities and motives could be determined later. Now, he must practice.

Whatever had controlled the sword released it. Larson executed the same strokes repeatedly, and all Gaelinar ever said was, "Again." The heat inspired by movement felt pleasant against the chill breeze, but it was night and time to join Silme and Brendor at the inn.

The practice went on until Larson's exertion no longer kept him warm from frigid winds. *Silme and Brendor have probably already gone to sleep,* Larson told himself. *And I'm stuck freezing my ass off with some maniac who thinks I'm still in boot camp."* Larson's patience wore thin as his tunic as the lesson dragged interminably onward.

"Enough!" shouted Larson. "You said we would go till night, not morning! It's time for a hot meal and a warm bed. This practice is finished!" He jammed Valvitnir into its sheath and stormed toward the inn.

"Wait," said the Kensei quietly. "There are two

minor mistakes I can correct if you perform the kata one more time. Then we will find you a warm bed."

Hesitantly, slightly embarrassed at his own outburst, Larson returned and unsheathed Valvitnir. Gaelinar stood an arm's length in front of Larson. "Go through the kata. I will retreat before you." When Larson's weight shifted to his leading foot, a sharp kick from Gaelinar sprawled him on the cold sand.

Larson clutched his knee, rolling from side to side. "What the hell! You god damned sonofabitch! I won't be able to walk for a week. Why . . ."

"If you listen, I will tell you why." The Kensei's face was a mask, but his eyes smiled broadly. And that annoyed Larson more than anything. "You have just learned two important lessons. First, do not put so much weight on your front foot. It's harder to defend, and if knocked away, you fall." He paused thoughtfully. "Also, never gainsay your teacher."

Gaelinar smiled and offered Larson his hand. With his assistance, Larson stood. "For the remainder of the evening, you are a friend, not a student. Let's see about your bed, hero."

Darkness had settled about swordmaster and pupil as they worked. The moon hung, little larger than her court of stars. Gaelinar crossed the sand and shouldered beneath the rope. "We'll talk on the way to the inn."

Larson limped after, only partially listening. For neither the first nor last time, he realized there was something unusual about his sword, Valvitnir. *Like some sort of primitive life form, it seems able to comprehend its environment and communicate with me in a rudimentary way. I just hope it knows how to fight.*

Gaelinar continued as Larson joined him on the roadway and they walked toward Ura's tavern. "I want to warn you about Silme."

Suddenly Gaelinar had Larson's full attention. Ideas swirled through Larson's brain, few plausible but all possible in this eldritch world which was not quite Old Scandinavia. Jaw set, he awaited the Kensei's words.

Gaelinar continued as the shapes along the roadside grew more familiar. "Silme and I . . ."

Larson squeezed his lids shut.

". . .visited her family today. I'm afraid Bramin reached them first."

Larson's eyes jerked open. They stood before Ura's Inn; the bar sign creaked as it swung in the breeze like a body from a hangman's noose. "What do you mean?" he asked, not daring to contemplate further.

"Killed, Allerum." Wind spread the tassels on Gaelinar's swords to a pair of golden flowers. "Faces twisted in pain. The bodies were dismembered and accorded none of the honor the dead deserved. Bramin left enough traces of sorcery for Silme to know without question." He added more softly. "As if we might mistake his evil for another's."

Larson shivered, chilled both by wind and the Kensei's words. He fought images of almond-skinned children screaming for fathers, fathers crying for daughters, women's last blood gushing rhythmically onto dirt floors. In Vietnam, the villains were not black-hearted half-breeds cursed with a demon inheritance, but true-blooded American boys who, hours later, would shed tears for an orphaned puppy or a fallen comrade. "Silme," Larson forced the question around his thoughts. "How is she?"

"Silme?" Gaelinar seemed puzzled by the query. "You mustn't forget, hero. She's not like most women. The Dragonrank training hardened her like the stone in her staff. And she's dedicated her life to neutralizing Bramin's atrocities. Come on." He caught Larson's hand and half dragged him toward the inn.

Trapped between two equally unsatisfying thoughts, Larson walled off his mind to a small square of consciousness. Like a man entranced, he let Gaelinar lead him to the inn, through a door behind the bar counter, up a narrow set of stairs to the door of their suite. The Kensei produced a brass key from the folds of his robe and inserted it in the lock. The door swung open to reveal a clean-walled room lit by a guttering lantern on a table surrounded by four matching chairs. Beside the lantern lay a bowl and pitcher. Cloth rags were spread neatly across the back of one of the chairs.

When the two men stepped into the room, details became more apparent between the spinning shadows cast by the lantern. The farthest wall was broken by four portals. Two were covered by drawn curtains. The others opened to smaller rooms furnished with beds of straw and cloth. Each held a night table with an unlit candle and a crude iron striker.

Gaelinar closed the door, crossed the room, and flicked his fingers through the water in the bowl. "Tomorrow, when we leave Forste-Mar, your real lessons begin."

Larson unlatched his sword belt and slung it across a chair. "Where are we going?" Frustrated by the elusiveness of the quest thrust upon him, Larson spoke his words as a challenge.

Gaelinar submerged both hands in the bowl and splashed water on his forearms. "Silme and I thought we should purchase a few more supplies in the morning." He examined Larson's torn and soiled garments with a disapproving frown. "Then," he continued in an apologetic tone which instantly turned Larson against the suggestion, "we thought we'd take you to the dream-reader."

"The what?" asked Larson suspiciously. His fingers massaged the pommel of Valvitnir where it rested on the chair before him.

Gaelinar scrubbed his face. "The dream-reader of Forste-Mar. She's an old witch with a few minor magics and a talent for mind search and thought interpretation. Silme thinks the lady might find some answers in that dream you had in the woods, something to explain your quest and send us in the right direction." He reached for a rag.

Though excited by the prospect of knowledge, uncertainty weakened Larson's grip on his sword. "What's the catch?"

Gaelinar tossed his towel aside and raised his eyebrows uncomprehendingly.

"What's this dream-reading process do to me? How does it work?"

"Do to you?" Gaelinar caught the sides of the bowl. "It doesn't do anything to you. And you might just as well bid me cast the protective circle. If you want to learn combat come to me." He patted his sword hilts. "For explanations of magic ask Silme."

Finding the answer unsatisfying, Larson scowled. Gaelinar lifted the bowl of water and carried it to a dented tin bucket on one of the chairs. As water splashed from basin to bucket, disturbing a thin film of oil which had settled on the surface, the Kensei softened. "Silme wouldn't suggest anything to hurt you. I think you know that."

Larson said nothing. So many times in Vietnam he placed his life in the hands of men whose morals he questioned. Now, he balked before the trust of the woman of his dreams and the man who gave his new being direction. "Yes," he admitted. "I know that."

"Good." Smiling, Gaelinar refilled the basin from the pitcher and left it on the tabletop. "Wash up and get some sleep. See you in the morning." He turned and strode through one of the portals, pulling the curtain closed behind him.

Gingerly, Larson removed his tunic, worn thin as a favored tee shirt though he'd owned it only three days. He moistened a rag and scrubbed his unfamiliar body, paying particular attention to his armpits, which were hairless, and his genitals which he had already determined looked normal by human standards.

Minor comparisons and benign memories of showers and flush toilets busied Larson's mind while he prepared for bed. But after he finished his scrub bath, gathered his tunic and sword belt, and settled into bed, thoughts descended upon him. He pictured a kindly old woman and a man stooped and tanned from years in the field. Between them, he imagined a snub-nosed boy, like his baby brother Timmy, and a girl beautiful as Silme, but with a wide-eyed innocence only youth can grant.

Larson fought the idea like madness, but he imagined the four again, crushed like roses after a broken romance. Blood colored the cold, stone floor. Limbs bent like fragile stems. Memory awakened, triggered others in a spreading circuit. Bodies sprawled in limp piles, pinned to walls in death, shattered to red chaos. Faces lay locked in permanent accusation, lacking ears, prizes claimed for the gruesome pride of death collectors. *And we were all death collectors.*

Larson kept his eyes open, letting the scenes wash across the rain-warped ceiling, waiting for them to play out and leave him the tranquillity of sleep. But peace remained elusive. Remembrance of Bramin's sorceries surfaced in a searing rush, and past horrors washed to a waste of grayness. Agonies Larson dared not wish upon Satan condensed to a dully throbbing reminder that Silme's family had experienced it all and worse. Surely death was the kindest of Bramin's atrocities.

Larson forced his mind to cheerier topics. He remembered his father and their yearly New Hampshire trips to hunt deer and grouse. But even then, his thoughts betrayed him. Larson recalled the phone call which pulled him from college midterms. His father had been killed, the victim of a drunk driver. He left nothing. To relieve their mother's financial burden, his older sister married, and Al Larson quit school to join the army. *I wonder if Mother knows I am dead.*

A noise startled Larson from his nightmare of memory. Relieved, he lay alternately sweating and chilled while his trained senses identified sound and location. He heard it again, coming from his left over toward Silme and Brendor. It was the gentle creak of floorboards beneath weight shifting with deliberate stealth.

Larson hit the floor in a crouch. His groping hands found his sword belt in the darkness, and he worked Valvitnir from its sheath without a sound. The blade trembled questioningly as he pressed it to his naked chest, hoping to shield the steel from residual light which might reveal him. Taking care that the inseams of his doeskin pants did not rub together, he pressed to the wall and worked his way toward the portal of his bedroom.

Again, Larson heard movement. Carefully, he flicked back an edge of his curtain and examined the main room. The lantern had burned out, and the suite lay in blackness. A light in the corner bedroom discolored its drawn curtain in a central circle, marred by wrinkles in the fabric. Beyond, Larson heard a sandal scrape wood and a pained human sob.

Larson stalked the sound, acutely aware of each of his own motions. Well aware any person skilled enough to harm Silme could easily kill him, Larson still continued, relying on surprise to even the odds. Positioned to spring, he snaked the sword forward and tipped an edge of the curtain up. The linen folded aside to reveal a slight figure pacing before a candle on a bed table. It was Silme.

Larson dropped his sword and stepped into the bedroom. Silme whirled abruptly. Her hair hung in a cascade of golden tangles, and her eyes looked red and swollen. A tear slid halfway down her cheek before she caught it with a finger and flipped it away. Though stripped of pretenses and pride, she seemed every bit as beautiful to Larson.

He caught her to his chest, and she, at first, resisted. Then grief broke in a flurry of tears. She wept for her family, for all the innocent victims of Bramin's hatred, and for the men of Midgard fated to die in Loki's Chaos. Her tears glided down Larson's chest. He pressed his arms around her, muttering senseless comforts. Her warmth raised him to a dizzying height of passion, and it took no small amount of will to suppress the urge to force his desires upon her.

Shamed by the lust incited by Silme's grief, Larson said nothing. Between sobs which shook the sorceress' body, he vowed vengeance on the red-eyed half-man responsible for her pain. For his own peace, he swore he would earn Silme's love and respect and one day bed the sorceress who was sapphire Dragonrank from Forste-Mar.

CHAPTER 4

Wolfslayer

"Brother fights with brother,
they butcher each other;
*   daughters and sons*
*   incestuously mix;*
man is a plaything
of mighty whoredoms;
*   an axe-time, sword-time*
*   shields shall be split;*
a wind-age, a wolf-age,
before the World ends."
                    —*The Spaewife's Song*

The dream-reader crossed the barren tract before her cottage and studied the main street of Forste-Mar through cataract-hazed vision. Four figures approached, too distant to discern through her aged eyes. Yet she identified her visitors without mortal sight. The woman at the lead glowed with a life aura bright as a barn fire, surely Dragonrank and therefore unmistakably Silme. Beside her walked a boy suffused by light so pale the dream-reader attributed the illusion to reflections of Silme's glory and her own near blindness.

Behind Silme strode her bodyguard of several years, the ronin, Gaelinar. To believe the rumors, he'd fought a thousand duels in the Far East without a loss and had been lured to the North by stories of fearless pirates commanding longboats carved in dragon form. No one knew how Silme had persuaded the Kensei to her cause, but his loyalty was beyond question.

The dream-reader knew the sorceress' last companion from gossip exchanged in the village market. The citizens named him a light elf. But even through diseased eyes which blurred Larson to an outline, the dream-reader found little comparison between him and the slight, giggling elves who whisked through her cottage on infrequent visits. His tread was heavy as a man's, his manner cautious and careworn.

As the four people crossed the ground before her cottage, the dream-reader lowered her head so her hood might keep her wrinkled face in shadow. She spread her arms. Wind caught the edges of her sleeves, drawing them from wrists thin as broom handles. Affectations were unnecessary before the sorceress, Silme, but the dream-reader assumed her position from decades of habit.

"Good day," called Silme a bit too loudly, as if the dream-reader's failing vision might affect her ears as well.

"Good morning, Lady Silme." The dream-reader bobbed her head once at the sorceress and again for Gaelinar. "Kensei." She waited patiently for Silme's introduction of the strangers.

"Lord Allerum and Brendor the . . ."

"Apprentice," Brendor interrupted in an excited squeak. "Silme's going to teach me my shave spell!"

Unable to discern expressions from her patrons' blurred faces, the dream-reader watched Silme's life aura for clues to her disposition. Now, the edges tinged pink with annoyance. Beside high rank Dragonschool, the reader's own aura seemed faded as the old cloak across her shoulders. "Have you come to visit an aging woman or for business?" asked the dream-reader, hoping for the latter. It was common knowledge Silme consorted with gods. Only desperation would drive Dragonrank to the lowly magics of a dream-reader. And desperation had its price.

"Business." Silme stroked the shaft of her staff thoughtfully. "Lord Allerum has a dream for your interpretation."

The dream-reader took one step forward and peered at Larson through slitted eyes. Closer, she recognized the small frame and angularity of an elf. But his long fingers balled nervously against the side of his breeches in a gesture uncharacteristic for a creature of faery. "I should gladly serve you, mistress." The dream-reader stepped around Larson. "In exchange, surely you have the power to cure an old woman's affliction." She pressed forward, giving Silme the full effect of her clouded stare.

Multi-hued light flickered briefly through Silme's aura. "Forgive me, lady. The spell you seek is within my power but not part of my repertoire. I can't help you."

Fearing to lose a chance at sight, the dream-reader persisted. "A mage of your rank has disciples. Surely one of them. . . ." She trailed to silence, awaiting the sorceress' reply.

Silme's life aura shimmered and swelled as she weighed alternatives. "The cost of spells for conjuration and exchange would exceed that necessary to heal you. They would weaken me."

The dream-reader said nothing, aware Silme's need for her services could bargain better than words.

"Even then," continued Silme, "I couldn't be certain the contacted wizard would agree to help you."

"I ask only that you try." The dream-reader tried to sound humble. "Nothing more."

"All right then," Silme responded in a hoarse whisper. She walked away from her companions and crouched on the frozen soil. Her life aura blazed like wind-stoked fire, then folded around her in a glimmering shield. Gaelinar strode forward and positioned himself before her, eyes watchful, hands tensed at his sides.

A slight smile shivered across the dream-reader's lips as she turned her attention to Larson. She shifted her shriveled hands to his shoulders. Sweat soaked through the fresh cloth of his tunic. He trembled slightly as a rising breeze flicked soft, pale hair and the folds of his newly-purchased silk cape against the reader's wrists. "Concentrate on your dream, so I can locate it," she informed him gently. "And try to lower your defenses."

The dream-reader knew her final suggestion was ineffectual routine. Only men accustomed to mental searches could withdraw defenses with any success. Thought invasion induced reflexive closure of the mind and its secrets. Anticipating a long session of relaxation techniques, the dream-reader thrust her consciousness toward the elf.

To her surprise, she met no resistance. Her mental probe passed effortlessly into Larson's mind, and his thought processes spread before her like the workings of a clock. It was not an elven mind; it lacked the wire-thin pathways and array of colors. It was a human mind and badly flawed. Passages looped in blind circles or linked with unrelated thoughtways in random binds and breaks. The effect seemed not unlike the looping chaos of stuffing from a torn doll. Though curious, the dream-reader avoided the strange conglomeration and focused on the faintly-glowing configuration which indicated Larson's present abstraction. Exploring other avenues of thought would betray the trust of her client.

The dream assumed the clarity of a play. The dream-reader saw the trees as Larson's link with the forest of his then current reality. The trunks muted to rivers, and Larson's memory of their names highlighted their importance to his vision. The titles which seemed foreign to Larson rolled through her mind like old friends: Svol the cool and Gunnthra the defiant, Fjorm and loud-bubbling Fimbulthul, Slidr the fearsome river of daggers and swords, Hrid, Sylg, Ylg, and Vid the broad, Leipt which streaks like lightning, and frozen Gjoll. These were the eleven rivers which cascaded through Midgard straight to Hel and the roaring cauldron of the spring, Hvergelmir.

The dream-reader of Forste-Mar saw the glowing form of the sword, Valvitnir, as the dream-Larson tossed it into the tumult of the Helspring. Hungrily, Hvergelmir swallowed the offering, and the dream-reader felt the relief inspired by the powerful being who had invaded Larson's thoughts and fashioned his vision. She found the misstep which caused the dream weaver to trigger unbidden memories of Vietnam and the misplaced circuits which amplified them to pain and awakened

Larson screaming. Gently, the dream-reader withdrew. She stepped away from her subject to face
Silme and Gaelinar.

Silme waited expectantly, her life aura dulled by
effort. "Within the week, expect a visit from an
aged wizard of amber rank. He has agreed to lift
your curse of nature."

Excitement plied the dream-reader like a faery
dance, but she resisted response for the sake of
dignity. "Bless you, mistress," she managed at
length. "And the elf's dream is clear. Some divine
being bid him on a quest to fling his sword into
the spring of Hel at the tip of the deepest root of
the World Tree."

In the silence which followed her explanation,
the dream-reader continued. "You must realize, I
can only interpret the dream. I can't guess who
inspired it, nor the motive behind the quest. Loki's
realm is unfit for any but the dead, and a journey
even to its borders unsafe for man or elf or god.
Legend says any object which falls into Hvergelmir
is utterly destroyed. Unless the sword contains the
essence of a most unholy creature, I can't fathom
why the gods would send the elf on such a task."

Larson seemed about to speak, then went still.
"How do we find this Helspring?" asked Silme
softly.

The dream-reader tugged her hood against the
wind. "North of town find the river Svip. Followed seven days it widens to Sylg which will bring
you, in several more days, to the valleys of darkness which lead to the underworld. Eleven rivers
coalesce before the golden bridge the dead must
cross to enter Hel. They join at Hvergelmir." Pity
rose for the four companions saddled with a quest
envied by no man. "Something strikes me odd

about pure gods sending minions to Loki's realm. If you'll forgive the advice of an elderly woman who has experienced more than most, the oracle of Hargatyr lies less than a day trip off your course. She can tell you whether destroying the sword will serve Midgard well or ill."

Silme's life aura guttered like an aging candle flame. "We thank you lady, for both direction and advice."

The men muttered gracious words. Then the four companions turned and made their way north-ward along the main track of Forste-Mar. The dream-reader watched until they passed beyond sight of her diseased eyes, and still she waited several minutes longer. Tipping back her hood, she let the breeze swirl her curled gray locks like sea foam. She loosed a single scream of joy and skipped toward her cottage for the first time since childhood. . . .

At the base of the spring, Hvergelmir, Loki paced before Bramin, his golden hair streaming like the mane of a lion. "We must stop them, Hatespawn."

"Stop them." Bramin's feral eyes followed his master's frantic course. "We have them routed straight for Hel, certain their mission is to destroy the sword."

Abruptly, Loki ceased pacing. "We have them headed straight for the oracle of Hargatyr."

"So?"

"So!" Loki screamed above the rush of falling waters. "So, the oracle taps the knowledge of the Fates for her wisdom. So she tells Silme and her wretched companions disposing of Valvitnir serves the cause of evil. Perhaps she even informs them of their true quest."

"Which is?"

Loki's face puckered into a frown of grim aversion. "Against our purposes, Hatespawn."

Bramin fingered his sword hilt, the fringe of his life aura dulled by irritation. "More specifically?"

Loki brushed off the half-man with a wave and resumed his rambling gait. "I'm a god! I've earned the right to be vague."

Bramin scowled, watching eleven rivers fuse in a cascade white as ice. "But not the right to grow impatient. That is your flaw. You told me so the first time we talked."

Loki froze midstride. His perfect features seemed chiseled and powerful as the background of clashing waters whipped to foam. He spoke in a placid monotone. "Very true, Hatespawn. You've more than enough time to divert them from the oracle, no matter the cost. Do you understand?"

Helblindi rasped from its sheath, sudden as a striking serpent. It drew shadow like a magnet, dulling the frigid waters and Bramin's life aura to gray. "Completely," said the Hatespawn.

. . . The dream-reader of Forste-Mar hummed a tune from her youth as she cleaned the floor of her one-room hovel with pendulous sweeps of a broom. Her gaze flitted from the black pit of the hearth, to the rectangle of her sleeping pallet, to the spindly-legged figure of her dining table. She imagined each piece of furniture as it had appeared before cataracts blurred her world to contours. Each hollow straw, every woodgrain seemed to reappear in the bold relief of her memory.

While the dream-reader basked in the anticipation of a visit from an amber-rank mage, light flared behind her accompanied by a thunderblast which shook the foundations of her cottage. She whirled. A tall, dark male poised before her. He clutched a diamond-tipped dragonstaff, and an ebony scabbard hung at his belt. A strikingly powerful life force bathed him in brilliance, its edge flaming red with anger. The dream-reader read murder in the undulating shadows which wound through his aura. She gasped. "Bramin?"

Bramin stepped forward. As he neared, the dream-reader recognized red eyes filled with accusation and the cruel sneer which twisted his features. Rage deepened his voice. "You trifling adept! Whatever galled you to meddle in my affairs. If you had contented yourself performing your paltry dream-reading abilities and not tried to second-guess my motives, I wouldn't have to take your life." His right hand caressed the hilt of his sword.

The dream-reader shrank from Bramin's threatening form; fear destroyed all pretense of dignity. "Bramin; please stop. I don't understand. . . ."

Bramin's sword slid from its sheath. Its blade scattered highlights of his life aura from the faded fabrics of the dream-reader's cloak. "I fashioned the elf's dream. The visions were yours to interpret, not to advise. You sent Silme to the oracle of Hargatyr!"

The permanent darkness of death loomed over the gray reality of the dream-reader's near blindness. She realized impudence would lose her any chance to claim Silme's payment, and tears blurred her vision further. Slowly, courage returned to her, lending her strength to speak against the dark elf. "And I would do so again. Silme has done only good for mankind. There was a time, Bramin, when you and your sister shared tea in my cottage. You both begged stories of magic. And, while the citizenry attacked your elven heritage, I protected you and warned them of your potential abilities. Does my loyalty gain me no mercy?"

Bramin's aura blazed red hatred. He advanced. The point of Helblindi hovered at the dream-reader's throat, driving her backward. "You just wanted my power," he accused. "You thought any kindness you showed me then would be repaid once I became Dragonrank. It was your investment, a gamble. You lost."

The dream-reader's back struck the wall with enough force to jar her fragile frame. The sword point scratched her neck. Desperately she thrust a mental probe to Bramin's mind, trying to understand the mad affliction which corrupted his thoughts and incited him to demonic fury. But her consciousness met defenses solid as stone.

Bramin's foot flicked against the dream-reader's knee, dropping her to the floor. "Grovel, witch!"

All strength fled the dream-reader. Gradually, panic drained to complacency, and she fixed an answering stare on Bramin. "Not for you or anyone else, Dark One. I'm too old to fear death."

Bramin gave no verbal reply. His face puckered to a scowl. Helblindi sheared through the dream-reader's throat. Pain wrenched a scream from her, but the half-man's laughter was the last sound she heard before the half-dead goddess, Hel, claimed her soul.

Deep in the forests north of Forste-Mar, near the banks of the river Svip, Larson repeatedly performed his only sword form for a Kensei who challenged him with offensive strokes of a wooden practice weapon. After four days of morning and evening lessons, the figures had grown as familiar to Larson as the never-ending sequence of pine and the widening river. Yet Gaelinar persisted, adding only simple directional changes to the basic cut of Larson's first session.

The time spent traveling between lessons might have offset the merciless repetition of Gaelinar's training had Silme chosen to grace Larson with conversation or even an encouraging smile. But she withdrew to inner contemplations, responding stiltedly to his attempts at humor, when she replied at all. During Larson's sword lessons, Silme and Brendor shared breakfast or dinner. After he finished, sweat freezing on his tired limbs, Larson was prepared for some social interaction along with his meal. But Silme would take Brendor into the woods for a discourse on magic, and Larson would have only Gaelinar for company. For reasons Larson could not discover, Silme appeared to be avoiding him.

I'll confront her today, Larson decided with unwavering resolution. *If I've done something to offend her, I've a right to know.* As his thoughts meandered in this new direction, Valvitnir jerked suddenly. Gaelinar's wooden sword rattled from the blade, skimming the edge of Larson's pants.

"Nice recovery." Gaelinar seemed pleased. "Perhaps you'll learn a new form tomorrow."

Larson flushed, too modest to credit himself with a maneuver wholly attributable to a sword it had become his mission to destroy. If the dreamreader was correct and Valvitnir housed the soul of an unholy being, it had thus far proved friendly.

Larson wondered whether the sword might lull
him to confidence and betray him in real combat.
Earlier, he had mentioned nothing of Valvitnir's
strange powers to Gaelinar since the sword rescued him from many embarrassing situations in
the course of the Kensei's teachings. Now, the
decision to confront Silme made him bolder.
"Gaelinar. I . . ."

He was interrupted by Brendor who crashed
through the thin tangle of brush, face glowing
with excitement. "Watch this!" called the boy.

Larson turned toward the child with a mixture
of relief and apprehension. Brendor's eyes screwed
tight in concentration. His face lined like an adult's.
His hand curled in a smooth gesture and shook
slightly, fingers stretched toward Gaelinar. "Shave,"
he said quietly.

Gaelinar flinched back. His chin, which had
sported a day's growth of stubble, was now clean
as Larson's. "Brendor, you did it!" screamed the
elf.

"I . . . did . . . it!" Panting with exertion, Brendor
cast his head about as if to determine which direction to run. "Shave, shave, *shave*, SHAVE!"

As the last command burst gleefully from Brendor's throat, hair sprouted from the Kensei's chin
in a stiff, unnatural beard. Gaelinar's face went
livid. Brendor loosed a strangled cry and staggered into the forest. Struck by the appearance of
his customarily neat and serious swordmaster, Larson broke into laughter.

"We'll continue in the morning." Gaelinar waved
a hand stoically. "Get something to eat."

Glad for the freedom, Larson wasted no time
on words. He sheathed Valvitnir hurriedly and
chased after Brendor, hoping the boy might lead

him to Silme. Eventually, he heard the sorceress'
voice, loud and angry, and followed it to a clearing near camp where Silme berated her apprentice without mercy. ". . . not a game, stupid child!
The summoning of a chaos force costs nothing; it
comes naturally to those born to magic. But you
know that channeling its energy to a specific enchantment drains power from its caster's life aura.
Your sloppy technique of partially focusing your
spell is all that saved you. Had you cast that second spell correctly as I taught you . . ." She paused.
Brendor quivered before her wrath like a towns-
man in the sights of a loaded gun. ". . . it would
have destroyed you."

Silme looked up as Larson entered the clearing,
and her glare made it obvious his presence was
unwelcome. Without so much as a gesture of greeting, she continued her tirade. "I was an idiot to
think I could trust a child with power . . ."

Larson wandered away, sick with frustration.
Now, when he had finally gathered the courage to
approach Silme with his feelings, she was busy
with matters she considered more important. Larson supposed hours would pass before she com-
posed herself enough to talk, and by that time she
would want to sleep. Crushed by ill luck, Larson
took a seat by the fire across from Gaelinar who
was scraping the last of Brendor's foiled attempt
at magic from his wrinkled cheeks.

Larson said nothing. He stared into flames orange as a sunset against the darkening background
of nightfall. After a short silence, Gaelinar sheathed
his dagger, pulled rations from a pack beside the
horses, and crouched at Larson's side. Apparently
sensing Larson's mood, the Kensei spoke with en-

couragement. "You've done well. You learn as fast as any I've taught."

Despite the value of Gaelinar's rare compliment, Larson merely watched the fire and made a noncommittal grunt. He saw little purpose in learning to wield a sword he was commissioned to destroy and even less in journeying with a beautiful woman who would never share his love. *Does the old man expect me to battle Bramin after a week of sword training?*

"Hungry?" Gaelinar spread a square of cloth before the fire and emptied a small sack of dried fruit and smoked meat.

Larson shared the food without tasting it. Gaelinar's words flowed about him, no more comprehensible than the bubblings of the river. At length, the Kensei stayed his wasted conversation and joined his companion in silence. The campfire settled as it consumed its supply of twigs. The moon rose like a chariot, a lingering token of the sun's glory. And still Larson brooded.

Gaelinar rose. He performed a dexterous series of katas, all lost on Larson whose thoughts centered on his own misfortunes. When the Kensei finished, he gathered bedding and spread it about the fire. He caught Larson's arm and gently tugged the elf to his feet. "Rest will do you good."

Larson made no protest but allowed himself to be led. He crawled between his own snug pile of furs; and, though he made no attempt to sleep, he fell prey to the blissful oblivion which veils men's burdens. Larson's peace was short-lived. He awakened to the low drone of Silme's voice beside him. Fearing he might lose another chance to talk, he groped toward the sound.

Larson caught Silme's leg in the darkness. She recoiled with a shriek. Magics fizzled to sparks around the sorceress, and Gaelinar's swords whisked from their sheaths in a defensive curl before her. "You stupid elf!" shrilled Silme. "You ruined my protection spell and weakened me for nothing. By Vidarr's shoe, am I surrounded by incompetents?"

Gaelinar flipped his katana and shoto to their sheaths and retook a position at Silme's side. "Excepting you, of course, Kensei," the sorceress muttered sullenly. She dropped her head, and again crafted the intricate enchantments of the circular ward which had defended them each night since Larson first met Silme and Gaelinar in the forest. Humbled, Larson retreated beneath his furs, sleep now an unattainable goal.

It's useless. Tears burned Larson's eyes while Silme's voice rose in incantation, followed by the crackle of intertwining magics. *I can't live with her derision, not after I've held her in my arms. Flawlessly beautiful, skilled, compassionate and strong, Silme personifies every quality a man could want in a woman. I would never have found one like her in the States. And,* he reminded himself, *I will never have her here.*

The coarse furs tickled Larson's cheek, and he brushed them aside with self-pitying fury. *I left my mother nothing but another life to mourn. As a soldier, I failed, only to be rescued from death for a task I still don't understand. I've duped Gaelinar with a living sword which learns his lessons better than I ever can. And Silme . . .* Larson gritted his teeth so tightly, his thoughts folded in a haze of redness. *As long as I remain part of it, this quest is doomed to failure.* He caught Valvitnir. With strength spawned of a boil of desperate emotion, Larson hurled the sword. It flew straight as a spear, struck the unseen enchantments of Silme's ward, and plummeted with a crash that woke every member of the party.

Cursing like a longshoreman, Larson sprang from his bedding and snatched up the sword. "I dropped it," he explained lamely for the benefit of his companions, though he doubted even Brendor would believe he was practicing at night with a sheathed weapon. But no one questioned Larson as he returned to his pile of furs and realized in a rush of self-deprecation he could not even desert the task with dignity.

A voice broke his dispirited train of thought. *Allerum.*

"What?" Larson responded with a growl, not wishing to talk. It occurred to him suddenly that the voice was unfamiliar, and his sinews snapped taut. "Who are you?"

"Did you say something, hero?" asked Gaelinar, apparently oblivious to the stranger's presence.

Gaelinar's lack of vigilance struck Larson as odd. The Kensei was usually the wariest member of their group. *Sssh*, hissed the first voice. *Don't talk aloud.*

What the hell, thought Larson. *Surely Gaelinar can hear as well as me.* But the swordmaster neither moved nor spoke again. Trusting Gaelinar's instincts more than his own failing sanity, Larson flipped to his other side and tried to sleep.

Allerum. I'm your sword.

Larson's eyes flared open.

Don't speak. I'm communicating through your mind. You need only think what you wish to say. Do you understand?

Larson's wits exploded into confusion. He lay with heart hammering. At length, he formed a tentative reply and concentrated on it with the intensity of a card in a magician's trick. *NO! AND WHO ARE YOU?*

You needn't shout! The response lanced through Larson's brain. *Just think normally.*

Whatthehell?

I am Vidarr, the silent god. Already I've sent more words to you than all my followers in the last century. From now, I answer only in images. Ask what you will.

Larson gnawed a fingernail, believing his insanity well beyond question. *My sword is a god?*

A scene unfolded in Larson's mind. Before him stood the figure of a man, blond as the citizens of Forste-Mar. His face was fair and creased by a smile. His clothing shimmered with an unearthly silver radiance. On his left foot, he wore a crafted sandal. On the other was an oddly-cobbled boot constructed of scraps melded without seam, though the artisan made no attempt to match color.

Oh my god! Fearing his exclamation might be some sort of blasphemy, he amended, *Sorry.* Growing braver he added, *The dream-reader called you an unholy being. And if you're a god, what are you doing in my sword?*

An overwhelming sense of exasperation filled Larson's head and transformed to grudging acceptance. His surface thoughts dimmed like lights before a play. Memory receded behind a presence which possessed his mind like a dream. From the perspective of the god whose image had recently occupied his thoughts, Larson marched across a meadow marred by the footprints of giant men. Beside him strode a figure more beautiful than Silme, though decidedly male. His face was clean-shaven and shaped without flaw. His hair hung in a golden mane of ringlets. Through Vidarr's perception, Larson knew the comely figure as Loki, and he watched the Trickster with contempt.

"Isn't it a glorious day, son of Odin?" Though

clear as chimes, Loki's voice held an edge of threat.
His slim hand stroked the hilt of an ebony-
scabbarded sword at his hip.

Vidarr gave no answer, nor did Loki expect
one. The Trickster adopted a look of suave assur-
ance, stopped suddenly, and slid the sword from
its sheath. The blade gleamed silver, then dulled
to black as light fled and shadow gathered along
its steel.

Unafraid, Vidarr frowned with impatience. He
knew his life was protected by Loki's vow to Odin;
the day had not yet come when one god could
directly cause the death of another. Reluctantly,
Vidarr examined the sword and found the crafts-
manship exceptional. He demonstrated his admi-
ration empathically and, when Loki sheathed the
blade, returned his aura to one of abhorrence for
his evil companion.

Loki laughed. "You like my brother and hate
me. Fickle, aren't you, Silent One?"

Confusion wracked Odin's son. He waited for
Loki's clarification.

Loki scuffed his feet in the dust, eyes dancing
with evil mischief. "By my magic, the soul of my
brother, Helblindi, resides in this sword."

Vidarr replied with tangible skepticism which
flared to accusation. Surely Loki's claim was ridiculous, a sacrilege from any but a deity of Asgard.

Loki stepped around Vidarr with the grace of a
cat, his cloak shimmering with enchantments. "Do
you doubt me, Lord of Silence? I can prove my
abilities well enough."

Vidarr followed Loki's movements with forced
indifference. Yet curiosity glimmered faintly through
his facade, and the Trickster seized upon it.

"I'd thought Odin's son too wise to judge with-

out evidence." His voice assumed the recrimina-
tory whine of a victim of injustice. "One demonstration will quell all doubt and clear my name.
Would you deny me that right?"

*It will take more than a display of magics to clear your
evil name*. Larson understood that Vidarr had kept
this thought to himself. The message the silent
god actually sent Loki was a mixture of impatience and reluctant concession.

Loki pressed his pale lips together and smiled
like a child with a secret. "If you'll help gather
materials, this task will be more quickly done. While
I find the many necessary components here on
the world of giants, I'd appreciate it if you'd pro-
cure some items from the dwarves. I'll need an
anvil and a piece of white metal more precious
than gold."

Before Vidarr could muster protestations, Loki
disappeared. To appease the Sly Trickster and
satisfy his own inquisitiveness, Vidarr traveled to
Nidavellir, the dark home of dwarves. Time passed
like a blur in Larson's mind, as if Vidarr tired of
the tale and condensed his adventures to outline.
He watched the silent god root through the par-
ings of dwarven blacksmiths for a fist-sized chunk
of platinum; then Vidarr hefted a half-ton anvil
and tossed it carelessly across his shoulders.

Returning at dusk to the world of giants, Vidarr
found his evil companion sitting cross-legged in the
dirt, head lowered and eyes glazed in trance. Vidarr
dropped the anvil; its impact tremored the meadow.
Loki took no notice. Words burbled from his throat
like boiling pitch. Orange light sprang to life, high-
lighting the Sly One in wicked splendor, a dancing
radiance of Helborn power.

Larson longed to shield his eyes from the glare,

but he was forced to witness the scene through Vidarr's eyes. Loki rose, and his aura flared green. "The metal?" Vidarr opened his hand, displaying his find. The platinum winked with reflected light from Loki's sorceries. "The spell works only . . ." Loki spoke gently, so as not to disturb the intricate mesh of his enchantments, "if the metal is carried by one burdened with a load of nine hundred-weight who then becomes . . ."

Loki's aura broke to a red explosion of fire. Sparks scattered in a wild arc and sizzled to oblivion against spring greenery. ". . . its victim!"

Too late, Vidarr realized his danger. Metal spun from his hand as he whirled to run. Magic pounded his back like a giant's fist and sprawled him over the stolen anvil. He struck the ground, body and soul sundered with a violent lurch. Larson felt his thoughts fold in blackness, spinning in the cyclone of Loki's fury. Oblivion strangled Vidarr's scream. There remained only a nothingness beyond darkness, the visual void of the blind accompanied by the ultimate silence of the deaf.

There followed a greater nothingness, a time of pure ignorance without benefit of discovery. From his prison of soundless, sightless eternity, Vidarr reached for the perceptions of those who molded his new blade form and plied the Fates for his destiny. But each attempt slammed him solidly against the impenetrable mental defenses of the gods and men who held him. Doomed to an existence without any contact with sentient beings, Vidarr settled uncomfortably into his confinement.

Claustrophobic panic nearly overwhelmed Larson's senses. Then Vidarr's awareness broke free to wander, unrestrained, through the mind of a future-born wielder selected by Freyr for his inability to defend against mental probes. Aside from a tangled web of guilt- and fear-inspired flaws mingled with strange words and concepts, Vidarr found functioning eyes and ears and a hand he could influence while it gripped his hilt. Larson realized Vidarr's window to the world was his own consciousness.

Larson felt violated. Remembering that the god could read his emotions directly, he struggled to control rising resentment and concentrated on a single question. *Why must I destroy you?*

For several seconds, Larson received no answer. The sword shifted uncomfortably in his grip as Vidarr abandoned pictures for words. *What makes you so certain Hvergelmir will destroy me?*

The dream-reader said . . .

The one who called me an unholy being? interrupted Vidarr.

Good point. Larson rolled to his back. Still clutching the hilt, he rested the sword across his chest and abdomen. *What does happen when I toss you in the Helspring?*

Uncertainty inundated Larson. Vidarr seemed irritated. *How should I know? Hopefully, it frees me. Only the Fates know the means to break Loki's spell, aside from the Trickster himself.*

The next question followed naturally. *So who influenced my dream?*

The hilt in Larson's fist went cold. *That, of course, is the problem. Apparently your people lost all means of mental exchange and warfare. You can't defend against manipulation. All your thoughts are suspect.*

Much of Vidarr's explanation meant nothing to Larson, but he had to agree with the final statement. *Why*, started Larson, trying to phrase the query delicately though he guessed Vidarr could read his intentions as well as his thoughts. *Why must we set you free?*

Reality crumbled before illusion as Vidarr again took control of Larson's mind, showing him the alternate fates of the world. Vision blurred to a vast white plain, and hail stung like cinders. Larson came to realize he was seeing a monstrous winter without end, a bitter frost which slew crops and beasts without mercy. Evil seized tree roots in a grip of ice, dropping century-old forests like stands of saplings.

As Larson watched in wonder, hordes of men appeared, arrayed in armor of skins, links, or chains. Shields gleamed on their arms. Axe, sword, and spear bobbed eagerly in the hands of warriors trembling like hounds before a hunt. Driven to madness by eternal cold, the armed men fell upon one another in a wild sea of battle without strategy, issue, or goal. Warriors dealt death to kin without remorse; men with matching crests fell, pinioned by each other's swords. Blood geysered, staining shields and snow like wine.

No! Larson bucked against Vidarr's control, ripped partially free only to fall prey to his own memories. The glint of light from metal became the flash of gunfire. War howls transformed to the roar of mortars. The scene broke to a tide of fire, and Larson screamed inwardly.

Intent on his demonstration, Vidarr seized a strand of Larson's sanity and hauled his charge back to his own imagings. The sun filled Larson's mind, a golden ball of glory shining down upon the chaos. From the sidelines, a wolf leaped upon the daystar, and caught it in fangs sharp as needles. Light crunched like bone, and bloody foam flecked the wolf's maw. The world plunged into darkness.

A distant cock's crow rose above the din of battle, followed by a second and a third. In blackness, the ground quaked. The World Serpent rose from its bed in the sea, and the gentle lap of surf became an all-consuming hell, battering rock to sand. Elsewhere, at the seat of the world, an enormous tree of ash moaned and shivered as a man and woman found refuge in the hollow of its trunk. Tension built like the crescendo of a song. While the men of Midgard slaughtered one another, greater armies gathered, preparing for a war which would color the heavens sunset red with the blood of giants, monsters, and gods.

The battle plain of Vigrid stood ready. Giants poured to its northern shore from a ship created of human fingernails. From a second vessel, Loki leaped to shore, leading the tortured souls of Hel who followed his commands like automatons. From the south came hordes of living flame led by the black giant, Surtr, whose sword blazed with the glory of the murdered sun. Before them all waited Loki's children: the flame-eyed wolf, Fenrir, breath soured by meals made of Midgard's warriors, and the World Serpent whose venom spewed as thickly as tar.

A handful of gods strode forth to challenge those who sought to destroy the world. They were flanked by the ranks of Valhalla, men who had died in the glory of war and whose souls had been rescued from battlefields by Odin for this conflict. Odin commanded his troop, terrible with his magic spear and helm of gold. The sight might have driven Larson to total mindlessness if not for Vidarr's influence. Guided by the god's vision, he saw the Silent One himself poised among the defenders.

With a howl of hellish fury, the Wolf sprang upon Odin. The warriors of Valhalla swept forward to meet the riot of giants and the Hel hordes under Loki. Sadly outnumbered but honed to a skill which evened the odds, their swords blurred to a whirling fury which scattered limbs and spilled lives like water.

Unable to turn from the violence, Larson pleaded for mercy. Despite his efforts to tear free, Vidarr's nightmare visions unreeled relentlessly. The battle raged on. Odin locked in mortal combat with the Wolf, whose fangs tore like daggers. Beside them, Freyr faced Surtr's firesword with only his fists for weapons. Freyr capered like a dancer, but a final lunge by Surtr tore open his gut. Larson watched helplessly as his patron became the first god to die.

Nearby, the World Serpent vomited poison on the taut-muscled god, Thor, who bruised the snake's mottled flesh with hammer blows mighty enough to fell an army of men. Thor crushed the Serpent's skull. The god stumbled nine steps in triumph, then collapsed, lifeless, as the venom overwhelmed him.

While parrying the strokes of giants, Vidarr searched for his enemy. He saw Loki's agile form dodge then return the blows of another god. Both sprang forward in offense. Sword scraped sword and each pierced flesh. God and Helmaster died together.

Vidarr broke from the throng. His cloak was stained with sweat and blood, his sword notched and dripping. As he raced to add his strength to that of his father, the Wolf swallowed Odin and turned on him. The scene progressed in slow motion. Eager for vengeance, the Silent God stomped his booted foot on the Wolf's lower jaw. His hands caught Fenrir's muzzle and held. Vidarr strained with an effort that taxed every sinew. Sweat sprang from his forehead, rolled down his cheeks like tears, and pooled on his lips. The Wolf loosed a human scream. Its body gave like cloth, sprouting a river of blood which washed souls from the battle plain.

The image froze as Vidarr's illusions ceased, the end slapping into Larson's mind with the impact of a broken film. Through the knowledge of a god, the elf knew that Loki had been defeated. Though Surtr's fires would destroy the world, elves, dwarves, giants, and most of the gods as well, there was a strong suggestion, like that in a fairy tale whose last sentence reads, "And they lived happily ever after," that all would ultimately be well. Somehow Larson knew the earth would rise again, complete with heaven and hell. From the two humans hidden in an ash tree would spring a new generation of men in the image of a god who was the son of a god; they would be the forebears of Larson's own world.

Just when Larson believed the nightmare had ended, Vidarr gathered his thoughts and forced him to understand what would happen if the same battle occurred with the silent god still imprisoned in his sword. Again the gods fought evil on the plain of Vigrid, but this time, the elf Larson had come to know as himself stood nearby, removed from the skirmish. As before, divinities died. Loki and the god fated to kill him locked in conflict. The glowing blue sword in Larson's grip quivered with sorrow as he watched Bramin wield Helblindi to protect Loki from his would-be slayer.

With Bramin's assistance, Loki endured until Fenrir swallowed Odin. But this time, Vidarr, Valvitnir *the wolfslayer*, shivered, imprisoned and impotent in the metal in Larson's hand. Alive because of the entrapment of Vidarr's soul, Fenrir howled with wolfish laughter and leaped onto Loki's enemy. With a snap of his jaws, the Wolf broke his opponent's spine then set upon the firelord, Surtr.

Loki rose in triumph. At his command, Chaos swirled like colored fire in a cyclone. It descended upon Vigrid, breathing new life into Loki's demon hordes. The souls of Valhalla fell prey to agonies beyond that which any being of flesh could understand. On Midgard, Chaos whipped men to killing frenzy. Fathers slew sons who pleasured mothers and raped sisters. Winds smashed rotted trees and swirled oceans to ship-swallowing maelstroms. Then Bramin's shadow sword splintered the World Tree, and the half-breed dragged the chosen survivors to the tortures of Hel.

"Stop!" Larson screamed through a haze of pain. "I've seen enough."

But the Lord of Silence showed him one thing more. Waves hurled foam against a cliff where Silme crouched, protected from the Hel hordes by a dwindling ring of magics. Larson watched helplessly as Bramin burst through her wards, his laughter cruel as thunder. "Now sister, your soul is mine!" He jerked the Helsword from its sheath and struck for Silme's breast. She flinched back; horror etched her features like sculpted glass.

"No!" Larson jerked away with enough force to break Vidarr's control. He fell back into his own private hell. A bullet-riddled, Vietnamese girl dropped to the ground screaming, her baby left to die in the field. A companion sprawled legless in the mud, babbling about returning home before medics shoveled him into a bag marked KIA. Shells screamed about Larson with the intensity of Loki's Chaos. Grenades roared like Fenris. Men fell like twisted puppets. *And this time it was his own hand on the trigger.*

Larson's fist struck the ground again and again. "Why me? Why me? Why me?"

This time, Vidarr did not answer.

CHAPTER 5

Childslayer

"Men fear death as children fear to go in the dark; and as that natural fear in children is increased with tales, so is the other."

—Francis Bacon, Of Death

Silme's voice cut through the dark haze of Larson's confusion. "Allerum! Allerum, what's the matter?"

Drawn from the wild surges of memory inspired by Vidarr's imagings, Larson raised his head. Gaelinar crouched among the pines, patient as a shadow in the predawn mist. Closer, Brendor and Silme stood over Larson. The child cocked his head sideways in question. Silme's brow was lined, and concern darkened her blue eyes. For the first time since they had left Forste-Mar, she regarded Larson with something other than hostility.

"Just another dream," Larson muttered. He rolled to a sitting position and refastened the sword to his belt. Sweat dripped from his hair.

Gaelinar grunted disinterestedly and returned to his bedding. Brendor comforted Larson in a childish soprano. "I have nightmares, too. I used to lie real close to Uncle Crullian and tell him about them. He said if I told someone, I wouldn't ever have the same bad dream again."

Now more accustomed to flashbacks, Larson recovered his composure quickly. He stared at Silme, both pleased and discomforted by her anxious expression. "Describe the dream," said the sorceress softly. "Your last vision detailed our quest."

"I don't think . . ." Larson trailed off. *Only a fool could surrender such an opportunity.* "Fine. But I want to talk to you alone."

Silme pinched her lip between her fingers. For some time, Larson received no reply except the low-pitched hum of mosquitoes. Eventually, the sorceress nodded assent and gestured toward the brush beyond camp. She passed through the sparse undergrowth with no more noise than a summer breeze. Apprehensively, Larson jumped to his feet and followed her into the twilight haze of the forest.

Once beyond sight and sound of their companions, Silme confronted Larson with silent forbearance. Though half-hidden in shadow, her face reflected the same distress Larson had recognized at his bedside. "The dream?" she reminded him politely.

"Dream," repeated Larson vacantly. Sunrise lit glimmers of gold in Silme's hair. Wind pressed the fabric of her dress tight against her finely-sculpted breasts. She held a pose of self-assurance and command, but her eyes imparted interest as well as concern. Suddenly Larson felt awkward as a teenager on his first date. "It seems I . . . my sword . . ." A rush of passion spoiled his composure. "Silme, I love you," he blurted without preamble.

Silme's lips parted slightly, but she said nothing. An answering warmth flashed through her eyes and quickly disappeared.

Caught in a swirl of joyous emotion at the realization that Silme might actually share his affection, Larson caught her to his chest. Her body went taut as wood against him. Her hand snaked free and lashed across his face. Larson staggered, as much from shock as pain and stared with wide-eyed innocence.

"How dare you!" Silme's indignation cut Larson like a blade. "I'll not suffer the touch of a rogue who would worry friends to maneuver a woman alone!" She whirled with an anger that whipped her hair in a golden wave and stormed toward the camp.

Crushed by Silme's rejection and sick with embarrassment at his brazen approach, Larson rubbed his aching cheek. As the sorceress stomped into the shadows, he called after her in a voice weak with humiliation. "Silme. Please wait."

She continued as if he had not spoken. The details of her retreating form became lost among the trees.

"Wait." Larson shifted from foot to foot and pressed his one remaining advantage. "I want to talk about Vidarr."

Silme hesitated.

Larson continued with a valiant attempt at resolve which could not hide his tension. "I know how to contact Vidarr."

Silme turned, too concerned about the fate of her god to ignore any source no matter how unlikely. Her manner was stiff and threatening as a crouched tigress. Yet her features held a stunningly feminine vulnerablity which awakened Larson's desires despite his attempts to hold his emotions in rein. "If this is another ruse, I swear I'll kill you," she said coldly.

From another woman the challenge might have seemed ludicrous, but Silme had proven herself quite capable of lethal magics. Larson shivered and pressed his lips in a noncommittal line. "It's truth. I've spoken with Vidarr."

Silme scowled warningly.

Quickly, Larson detailed his story, the sequence of mixed reality and illusion which had threaded through his mind since nightfall. As he spoke, Silme's pinched face relaxed to nearly accepting warmth. But her arms remained crossed, and her fists tightened against the fabric of her cloak. From the corner of his eye, Larson caught Silme staring at him with strangely tender sympathy. But whenever he met her glance, she turned her face away like a star-struck school girl found examining the object of a crush.

"So you see, Vidarr's been with us all along." Larson swallowed, both confused and intimidated by Silme's odd behavior. "I guess I can't expect you to believe me. I'm never quite certain when to believe myself. I . . ." Larson stopped speaking as he realized proof swung from his hip. He pulled Valvitnir from its sheath so abruptly Silme recoiled. "Here. Speak with him yourself." He offered the hilt to the sorceress.

Larson's mind tingled from a blast like static. An idea glided gently though his thoughts. *Allerum. You're the only one who can communicate with me.*

"What!" Larson screamed aloud. Silme startled

again. "What do you mean?" he challenged the sword.

"I . . . I said nothing," Silme stammered.

Silme's mental defenses are too strong for my intrusions, Vidarr explained. *I told you before. You lack mind barriers. That's why Freyr chose you.*

Damn. Larson returned the blade to its scabbard, hand heavy against its jeweled hilt. *Now what do I tell Silme?*

"Allerum. Are you well?" Silme reached for Larson. He cringed reflexively, though her touch was gentle on his shoulder. "What's happened?"

"Vidarr can only speak with me." Grieved by his discovery, Larson did not notice the change in Silme's demeanor. "Now you'll never trust me." He spoke more to himself than to the sorceress. Then, in a rush of emotion, he continued quickly, "I suppose I really can't blame you. But I've loved you almost since the day we met. When I told you how I felt, hope made me think you returned my affection. I'm sorry I grabbed you, Silme. It was all a stupid misunderstanding." Larson gathered a great breath and released a sigh so loud it nearly obliterated Silme's whispered answer.

"There was no misundertanding."

Larson caught his breath. "What did you say?"

Silme met Larson's gaze for the first time since he'd confronted her in the brush. "I do love you. I . . ." She turned away with a lowered head, her face buried in her palms.

Larson hovered, uncertain. He wanted desperately to hold and comfort Silme, yet memory of her warning stayed him. Touching the sorceress against her will could well prove fatal.

Silme looked up. Her eyes were miserably red,

yet tearless. "Someday," she began with an obvious attempt to be tactful. "I want to have children."

Confusion strained Larson's smile. "That would suit me, too."

"But it can't be with you," Silme continued. "And we mustn't start something we can't finish."

Larson opened his mouth, but found himself unable to speak. He stared at Silme's face which seemed to shine like a second sun as dawn dispelled all darkness but the shadows of trees and ferns.

"You don't understand." Silme seemed troubled by his ignorance.

Larson stroked his sword hilt while he searched his mind for a reply.

"You're an elf," Silme prodded softly.

It always seemed such a simple thing to remember, yet Larson continued to forget he was no longer a man. Doubts rushed upon him like a plague. Once before he had wondered whether elves and humans could interbreed, a question pushed aside by the many adventures and wonders of Silme's world. Now, if he was to believe the sorceress, their union was impossible. But even through a haze of frustration and sorrow, Larson discovered a flaw in his conclusion; he wondered why Silme attempted to dupe him with biological falsehoods. "I may be from another world, but I'm not a fool. I know elves and humans can have children together. Your half brother . . ."

Silme wrung her hands with a fresh aura of distress. "That's the problem, don't you see?"

"No."

Silme paced. "Our children would be half-breeds like . . . Bramin."

"No!" Larson's denial held the authority of a

command. "Bramin's father was a *dark* elf. *His* demon blood ruined your brother."

Silme stopped, shaking her head vigorously. "Bramin was a good child until the gibes of neighbors poisoned him. Our offspring would fare no better. This world is unprepared for crossbreeds of any type. I'm sorry, Allerum." Resigned, Silme turned and walked solemnly toward camp.

"Wait!" Larson's screamed order stopped Silme in her tracks. "Denying love won't make it go away. You can't turn it off and on like a light switch!" Afraid to speak too boldly and anger Silme, Larson pursed his lips and kept the remainder of his thoughts hidden. *How can you condemn the citizenry of Forste-Mar for their treatment of Bramin when your own prejudice transcends love?* Desperately, he continued, "By his appearance, Brendor's a half-breed of Scandinavian and some darker race. And Gaelinar's a goo . . . a full-bred foreigner."

"Light's witch?" Silme seemed confused by Larson's tirade. She folded her arms across her chest and did not bother to face him. "They're both human. And Gaelinar can silence teasing."

"So can we." Larson's voice cracked as he sought to make his point before he lost Silme forever. "We can protect our children."

Silme pursed her lips and said nothing. Nor did she move when Larson came up behind her and made his final plea. "I'm good enough for your god, Silme. Why else would Freyr have chosen me to save him?"

The sorceress turned slowly. "And once we free Vidarr, every human in Midgard would respect us and our offspring."

Larson stared, not daring to believe the uncertainty which softened Silme's tone. He met her gaze. Warmth replaced the menacing coldness which had marred the beauty of her eyes. He caught her to his chest. Her presence drove aside all memory of the biting winds. She returned his embrace wholeheartedly, without trace of her former reluctance. Her slim hands sent shivers of desire through him, inducing his mind to conjure a third world between the archaic fantasy of Midgard and his nightmares of Vietnam. It encompassed only Silme and himself, a slim shadow of reality which would hazard no intruders.

Wind ruffled the foliage which defined the clearing, but Larson remained blind and deaf to everything except Silme. He wound his fingers in the soft waves of her hair, savoring her beauty now promised to him by love. Silme's hesitation changed his existence as suddenly as had death. Since his enlistment, the bliss of sleep melting to reality each morning filled his mind with dread. But from now, the rising sun must reawaken euphoric memories of Silme. And even after the initial intensity of their relationship faded, Silme's fierce loyalty to causes would bind them for as long as an elf and a sorceress might live.

Thrilled to the elation of love long denied, Larson pressed his lips to Silme's and explored her mouth with his tongue. He desired to know her like a treasured story which, read a thousand times, would never lose its magic. He studied her with his eyes, hands, and mind, dreading at any moment that she might stiffen and grow cold to him. But it never came. Silme's answering warmth intensified their kiss until Larson withdrew for fear of losing control of his passion so close to camp and driving Silme away with boldness. *She loves me!* Joy exploded within him.

Gradually, Larson's narrow ribbon of world expanded, and realization crowded him. He recalled Silme's earlier reluctance and her words which seemed so simple yet nearly formed an impenetrable wall between them. *Someday, I want to have children.* The accusation in her voice triggered memories, plunging Larson deeper into his flawed mental tapestry. Poised at the edge of sanity, he brushed aside the plaintive visages of slant-eyed orphans. The effort flung him further into his past to an age when he welcomed rather than feared the night. Though discomforting, his vision held none of the terror usually inherent in flashback. Soft and vague as a whisper, he revived the porcelain doll features of his young brother, Timmy, as they sat before the headstone of their father's grave. The haze of gathering night hid the tears in the child's eyes, but his voice emerged as a quavering whine. "Why? Why did he have to die? Why would he go to heaven and leave us?" His plea faded in the stillness.

In his memory, Al Larson scuffed his shoe in the dust, fighting his own sorrow for an answer. "He loved us, Timmy. God took him . . ." *God and his drunk driver.* Larson's present thoughts twisted the past. ". . . Dad didn't want to leave us. No one chooses to die." *No one but an enlistee.* Again, the Larson in Midgard amended his imaginings. This observation opened other channels of memory. He recalled the day he left for boot camp, plagued by doubts yet morbidly excited by the glamour of espionage and the challenge of matching wits with other men. While in a zone of peace, distant dangers enticed him. But this thrill shattered before the hollow glare of betrayal he found in Timmy's eyes. Larson realized suddenly his brother had never said "good-bye."

A tear formed in Larson's eye, blurring his image of Timmy. Joy fled before an onrush of resolve. *Lost in the promise of passion, I dared to believe I could raise a child. I cannot subject some kid to my insanity or the consequences of flashback. Every person I care for becomes a weapon for my enemies. A child will not join my life until I learn to control my thoughts. And I can't allow myself to love Silme until we vanquish Bramin.*

Larson dropped his hands to his sides, and his index finger traced a gem in Valvitnir's hilt. Vidarr's voice crashed into his mind. *You hypocrite! Now who thinks of controlling love? Are you selfish or merely stupid?* Anger speared through the pathways of Larson's mind, and he winced beneath the onslaught of emotion. *Denying love won't protect you from grief. And fatherhood is more than ancestry. You already have a child; Brendor cares deeply for you. Does the camaraderie you shared in Forste-Mar mean nothing to you? If you reject Brendor like you did Timmy, you'll destroy his trust completely.*

"Allerum?" Silme caught Larson's arm.

Larson shoved the sword hilt aside; and Vidarr's presence fled his mind, leaving ghostly echoes in its wake. *I never abandoned Timmy! I did what I had to do. Do you think I wanted to go to war?* He battered aside the nagging memory of his brother's face, replaced it with others: his sister Pam, Ti Sun, Brendor. Each had experienced the greatest trauma chance could perpetrate upon a child, the loss of a parent. Like Timmy, all three returned to life with a resilience Larson could scarcely comprehend, innocents caught in a world without mercy. *They came to me with trust and hope. And I betrayed them all!* "Damn it, I do love Brendor. He needs me. He shall become our first child."

Silme seized Larson's hands and chided gently. "Of course we will raise Brendor. Did you think I'd abandon a partially trained apprentice who knows just enough of magic to endanger himself?"

Not realizing he had spoken aloud, Larson shied. Relaxing, he smiled. Again he pulled Silme to him, content with the pressure of her body against his. His thoughts remained in a lazy stupor of complacence. Stolen in death from a world at war, Freyr seemed to have given him everything: life in a new world, a woman more beautiful than a fairy-tale princess, and a child who, if a bit inept, reminded him of himself in youth and might one day inherit great power.

Silme continued speaking softly in his ear. "Naturally, I still think it best to leave Brendor safely in a town until our conflict with Bramin is completed. A battlefield is no place for a boy."

Larson agreed. Before he could reply, Gaelinar's gruff baritone interrupted their embrace. "Allerum. Time for your lesson."

Muttering blasphemies from his own world, Larson released Silme. He knew from past experience it was as unhealthy to ignore Gaelinar as a rearing cobra. For several seconds, the elf stood, touching only Silme's fingertips. "See you at breakfast?"

"Of course," she replied as if that had always been her habit. Hand in hand, they returned to camp.

Sunlight spilled through the clouds, coloring the river Sylg like gilt. But Larson was too preoccupied to notice. Feet soaked by dew, he followed Gaelinar's instructions with a renewed enthusiasm which pleased his teacher. "Good, Allerum. You've learned to treat your sword as a friend rather than an obstacle. Again."

Laughing inwardly at the unwitting double meaning of Gaelinar's praise, Larson repeated the maneuver. Valvitnir crashed solidly against the Kensei's notched wooden blade. Momentarily, Larson's attention strayed to Silme who watched his practice with approval.

"Enough." Gaelinar followed the direction of Larson's stare. "Work will make a swordsman of you. For now your interests are elsewhere."

Smiling, Larson sheathed his sword. Drying sweat intensified the late morning chill as he strode to Silme and took her arm. Returning to the campfire, they found Brendor sorting a sack of rations.

The four travelers breakfasted together for the first time in more than a week. Glad for company, Brendor prattled in an unending, childish banter. More attentive to Silme's hand, Larson heard little of the conversation until the sorceress spoke. "Yes. Brendor's done well. He's learned the spell I promised to teach him."

The child beamed as Silme continued. "I recognize this land. The town of Manivoll lies a half day ahead. I have friends there who would gladly watch Brendor while we complete our quest."

Brendor's smile vanished, replaced by a grimace of horror. "Watch . . . you can't leave me! You just can't, I . . ." His eyes pleaded with Larson.

Gaelinar nodded in tacit agreement with Silme's plan. Unable to meet Brendor's eyes, Larson took a sudden, inordinate interest in his meal.

Brendor leaped to his feet. His unfinished apple tumbled to the dirt. "I won't go! I won't go! I won't . . ." When this tactic gained no sympathy, the child changed to another. "Allerum." He knelt beside Larson and seized the elf's arm with grubby fists. "Please, Al. Pleeease."

Larson closed his eyes as the image of another child took vivid form in his memory. Ti Sun's voice rang clear as reality. "Candy, Joe?" A small hand tugged at his fatigues.

Larson heard himself reply, his voice stiff with feigned offense. "You know my name, Ti Sun."

The child amended. "Candy, Al. Please, Al. . . ."

"All right. Okay." Larson thrust a hand into his pocket and retrieved a packet wrapped in crisp, clean paper. Ti Sun watched with a bright-eyed excitement which made Larson smile. Slowly, he peeled away the wrapper to reveal a piece of chocolate melted nearly to liquid.

"Thanks! Thanks!" The child accepted the offering and soon coated his fingers and mouth with candy.

Gavin called from farther along the road. "Al, you coming?"

Larson turned. Light flashed through his thoughts like a warning. Suddenly, he realized he was caught in flashback as fully as a shallow sleeper knows when he is dreaming. Memory crowded him, solid as brick. Larson struggled against reexperiencing the catastrophe he could not bear a second time. He tried to force his mind from Ti Sun a dozen times with no success. Madness engulfed his conscious thought, pushing his mind back toward a village in Vietnam and the chocolate-stained child with the beatific smile.

Larson staggered. His hand cracked painfully against steel. Inadvertently, he seized Valvitnir's hilt, and another consciousness merged with his own. With Vidarr's aid, Larson escaped his flashback none the worse for his vision except for sweat-slicked palms and a shiver which wracked his entire body.

Brendor clung to Larson's shirt, his entreaties muffled by folds of cloth. Larson mentally communicated profuse gratitude to Vidarr, then turned his attention to the child at his chest. "Brendor, I like you very much."

The child tightened his grip.

"Enough so," Larson continued, "that I want to keep you as a son." The words sounded hollow to Larson's ears. Even nine months in Vietnam had not aged him enough to have a ten-year-old child. *Al Larson was only twenty, but I can't know the age of this elf body in which Freyr placed me. According to fairy tales, elves are immortal. If that holds true, the point becomes assuredly moot.* Larson forced his thoughts from this new distraction. "I won't have you killed because of my task. You stay in Manivoll, Brendor. I won't apologize for caring enough to keep you safe."

Brendor made no reply, but his mouth puckered to a scowl and he moved away with a tread sufficiently heavy to convey betrayal. Haunted by remembrances of a Vietnamese boy who became a casualty in the affairs of men, Larson paid the sorceress' apprentice no heed. He helped Silme and Gaelinar pack the horses, believing his decision a wise one.

The journey to the town of Manivoll convinced Larson of the soundness of his choice to side with Silme and Gaelinar. In an attempt to sway the lenient elf who had already proven himself a child's easy mark, Brendor became Larson's self-appointed servant. The boy volunteered to carry Larson's supplies on his own horse, dismounted to retrieve a cape pin the elf dropped, and offered to groom all the steeds at their next encampment. Larson supposed Brendor would have eaten, drunk, and pissed for him if given the opportunity. Since Gaelinar recognized the change in Larson's and Silme's relationship, he rode ahead on the pretext of scouting; but Brendor's constant presence made even simple exchanges of affection impossible. By the time the travelers reached the outskirts of Manivoll, Larson could scarcely wait to be free of the boy.

Brendor fell distressingly silent as they entered the town. Larson recalled the first time his mother had left him in the home of a strange babysitter. Then, he had clung to his mother, overwhelmed by the irrational fear she would never return. Sensing his discomfort, his mother had entrusted him with a necklace she wore every day. Though it was senseless to think she would abandon him and not her jewelry, the gesture consoled him. At the time, Larson had been considerably younger than Brendor; he knew a token far more valuable than a silver chain would be required to reassure the healer's nephew.

The moment Larson and his companions reached the town proper, peasants converged on Silme like groupies in the presence of a rock star. Disquieted by the gathering crowd, Larson, Gaelinar, and Brendor shied away from the sorceress' admirers. The Kensei explained in a whisper. "Years ago, Bramin sent a dragon after Silme. After a long and arduous battle, she defeated the wyrm near the town of Manivoll. Naturally, the citizenry was convinced she rescued them from the beast; and in all fairness, she probably did. Once Silme recovered from her confrontation, she hired me as bodyguard."

Larson nodded, only partially listening as he pondered a means to comfort Brendor. His only item of value was Valvitnir, but he could not hand the sword to the boy and still complete his quest. Gaelinar's katana and shoto were surely off limits; and Larson doubted Silme would surrender her dragonstaff to a novice magician, though she often left it in Gaelinar's care.

A tarp-covered wagon creaked past Larson and stopped before the throng which surrounded Silme. A man reined in the horse while a plump woman dragged a freckle-faced girl toward the sorceress who was already engaged in an inordinate number of simultaneous conversations. A gust of wind swirled a few dusty feathers from the wagon, and the woeful clucks of its live cargo gave Larson an idea. He placed an arm about Brendor's slumped shoulders and addressed the Kensei. "How many days of travel do we have left?"

Gaelinar kept his gaze on Silme, though she surely had nothing to fear from her reverent crowd of townsfolk. "A half day to the oracle and the same back to the river. Then one more day to the Valleys of Darkness and the Helspring."

"And another to return to Manivoll for Brendor," Larson finished. "How much food do we have?"

Gaelinar scratched his leg through the layers of his wind-spread robes. "Four, maybe five days."

"Good," said Larson with surprisingly effective finality. "Just enough to reach our goal and get us back to Brendor. We won't buy any rations here." He smiled at the child. Without supplies or a nearby town, Larson and his companions would be forced to return to Manivoll to secure food or go hungry.

Gaelinar looked away from Silme to confront Larson. His glower made it clear he understood Larson's intentions, and equally apparent that they displeased him. "We may be delayed."

Larson remained adamant. "Unless we're killed, we can make it back in five days."

Gaelinar rattled his fingers against the sheath of his katana impatiently. "I consider death a more extreme delay." He met Brendor's stricken stare and relented. "Fine, no rations. But I'm certain Brendor knows I could think of better ways to be rid of a young wizard than leaving him in a town, with my name and description, to wreak future vengeance." Gaelinar patted his sword pommel to make his pronouncement perfectly clear. Still staring at the boy, the Kensei pointed at the adoring peasants and changed the topic. "Brendor, Silme has many friends in Manivoll. If you ever wanted to become a silversmith or a baker or a cooper, let her know."

"I want to be a wizard." Brendor's pout was uncompromising.

"And?" Gaelinar asked as if the child had not finished.

"Just a wizard." Brendor jerked his head with resolution. "Wizards are the smartest people in the world."

Gaelinar laced his fingers on his chin as he pondered a situation which had grown more complex than he anticipated. Larson tried to help. "What's so special about wizards?"

Brendor answered without hesitation. "Wizards make magic, and they know more than anyone else."

"More than silversmiths and coopers?" Larson asked, though he was unfamiliar with the latter occupation and could only guess at its meaning.

Brendor nodded.

Larson winked at Gaelinar. "Then I guess you already know how to fashion jewelry and . . . um . . . shoe horses."

"Well . . . no."

Gaelinar chuckled at Larson's misinterpretation of a cooper's profession. "Did your Uncle Crullian know how to . . . um . . . shoe horses?"

Brendor bit his lip and nodded assent.

"As does Silme," Gaelinar finished. "Wizards are supposed to understand simple things like that." He cast a furtive glance toward Silme who had already begun working her way toward them through the crowd. The Kensei's voice dropped to a whisper as he addressed the child again. "Lucky for you Silme never discovered the gap in your education or she wouldn't have let you become her apprentice. You've only five days to correct your serious deficiency. But don't worry, we won't tell her." The swordmaster clamped a hand over his mouth in mock conspiracy as Silme dispersed the throng and returned to her companions.

"We won't have any problem finding a temporary home for Brendor." Silme jabbed the road dirt with the base of her dragonstaff. "I've found more than enough volunteers."

Gaelinar winked at no one in particular. "Brendor has requested a five-day apprenticeship with the blacksmith."

"Fine choice," she said to the boy. "I'm certain Sigurdhr would appreciate your company." She led her companions through a town smaller and poorer than Forste-Mar, stopping occasionally to exchange greetings and introductions. Larson met scores of blonds and redheads with names which required spelling out. He found that most had final pronounced e's or silent r's and promptly forgot all of them. For their part, the townsfolk spared Larson more than his share of stares, but he recognized none of the hostility against elves

he had received in Silme's hometown. He wondered how much Silme's presence might have al-
tered the events in Ura's tavern.

Larson heard the crash of hammer against anvil
long before they rounded the corner of Sigurdhr's
house. They found the blacksmith intent on a
bent strip of steel, his honey-colored beard sweat-
plastered to his chin. Back to the newcomers, a
youngster a few years older than Brendor worked
the bellows with an effort which grew sloppy with
fatigue.

"Yo, Eirik!" Sigurdhr bellowed at the boy. He
raised his head, caught sight of Silme, and stopped
in mid-yell. "Silme!" He gestured her forward with
an exaggerated wave. Sigurdhr examined his works
briefly, dismayed to find only horseshoes, barrel
hoops, and a wood-cutting axe, none of which
seemed the proper gift for a lady. Eirik released
the bellows with a relieved sigh and shook cramps
from his arms.

While the blacksmith introduced his son, Eirik,
and Silme presented her companions, Brendor
clung to Larson despite the fact that the elf was
every bit as inexperienced as himself. Eirik greeted
Brendor with so much exuberance, the healer's
nephew regained sufficient confidence and interest to release Larson and speak. "I'm a wizard!"

Eirik's features twisted in awe. Sigurdhr nodded
encouragement. "Silme. You and your distinguished
companions must stay for dinner and the night.
Kelda's prepared lamb stew with goat's milk cheese.
She always makes enough for a boat load of warriors. And we've plenty of room." He waved his
guests toward the door of the cottage without
waiting for confirmation.

For the first time, Larson noticed the streaks of

gray in the sky which heralded sunset. The gnaw-
ing in his gut which he had attributed to the
anxiety of entering the town became a tense grumble of hunger. They had traveled right through
without pausing for lunch. Eagerly, he followed
Silme and Brendor through the cottage door, into
the welcoming aroma of gravy and fresh-baked
bread.

Gaelinar bowed politely to his hosts. "Forgive
me, Sigurdhr Blacksmith. Lord Allerum and I
cannot attend your meal. We've a sword lesson to
complete."

Larson turned suddenly and reluctantly from
the feast. "Now? But there's food on the table."

Gaelinar bowed again, but his words were without compromise. "Practice. Now."

"Excuse me," Larson mumbled to their host. He
found abandoning dinner for swordplay painful,
but he followed the Kensei across the brown grasses
of the blacksmith's lawn to an open area beyond
the forge. An edge of the sun had already slipped
beneath the horizon, coloring the western sky as
red as the blood in Vidarr's vision. Larson scowled
as he reached for his sword. "You're one hell of a
gung ho gook."

"Pardon me?" Gaelinar's hand paused on the
brocade of his katana.

"Nothing." Larson sighed, enjoying the sound
of English in this legendary Northern world. "But
where I come from, it's impolite to refuse dinner
with a host."

Gaelinar nodded once, his eyes dark as mid-
night. "Hero, if you miss a meal tonight, you will
have another tomorrow." He paused as the air
hummed with the first of the evening's mosquitoes. "If you skip practice, you may not. Begin."

Larson obeyed with reluctant annoyance. In two days, he would face the greatest challenge of his new life with nothing but the knowledge of a few dodges and strikes. Surely one lesson more or less would make little difference to his abilities. But Gaelinar seemed to think otherwise, and Larson found it impossible to argue with the swordmaster concerning his own trade.

Gaelinar worked Larson without mercy far into the moonless night. For each success, the Kensei presented a new challenge until Larson's annoyance folded beneath all-encompassing fatigue. More and more frequently, he relied on Vidarr's cues. By the time the practice concluded, without ceremony or praise, Larson no longer wanted food, just a place to lie down and a full night's rest.

Gaelinar and Larson returned to the cottage in a silence which pleased the elf. Condemning words or maxims would have rekindled the exasperation he struggled to suppress. Inside, Gaelinar joined the conversation of Silme, Sigurdhr, and Kelda who shared tea before a roaring fire. Larson excused himself with a yawn, and Kelda showed him to a bedroom with a straw pallet and a hand-knitted quilt. There, Larson promptly fell asleep.

The dream seized control of Larson during the shallow, twilight slumber near to awakening. It began as a pleasant vision of the extension of their journey. Gaelinar, Silme, and himself rode along a meandering path beside the river Sylg, which twisted like a silver serpent, widening to a torrent of ice-flecked waters. The trail forked many times. Always in the past they had taken the branch which most closely paralleled the river. But in the dream, Silme indicated a wooden sign corroded by fungus and started down a side path which led away from the stream.

As the dream-Larson turned to follow, panic seized him like an overdose of adrenalin. He dismounted and dropped to a crouch, heart hammering in his chest. His mouth dried to rawness. His vision blurred to haze. War memories pressed toward expression, but the being who inspired his nightmare wove barriers with the intricacy of a spider. In the vision, Larson shook his head with uncharacteristic violence and gestured toward the northern trail along the river Sylg.

There was no sound in Larson's dream, but when Silme cleared slime from the road sign, its writings became clear:

Temple to Odin
The Oracle of Hargatyr

With an air of exasperation, Silme and Gaelinar reined their horses down the eastward branch. Reluctantly, the dream-Larson remounted and followed, but with each hoof-fall his anxiety trebled. Rows of twisted juniper passed unnoticed. The scenery might have been painted backdrops for all the heed he paid it. Instead, his attention focused on the looming gray outline of the temple to Odin.

By the time Larson and his companions reached the temple dooryard, his clothing had adhered to his sweat-soaked torso. He paused, studying the squat structure with an aura of mistrust. Brown ivies swarmed its exterior in uneven clumps, making it seem to lean awkwardly to the left. Moss chinked the wall stones like green mortar. Larson almost expected to see lightning flare between nonexistent watchtowers. He shivered, wondering whether to blame the temple's eerie appearance or his heightened senses for the fear which coiled

his muscles nearly to immobility. He felt like a
traitor who had refused both cigarette and blind-
fold before the firing squad.

At Silme's knock, the ancient door swung open
with a squeal of complaint. A half dozen drab-
robed acolytes met Larson and his companions
and escorted them past stained altars. Beyond, a
dark curtain crisscrossed with glimmering silver
threads spanned a doorway from ceiling to floor.
Gaelinar and Silme passed through a slit in the
fabric. Larson followed them into a room as gray
as the moment before dawn. At its farthest end sat
the oracle of Hargatyr, a young woman with a
seemingly endless cascade of reddish hair. Though
shadowed beyond recognition of detail, her face
seemed not quite normal to Larson. Before her
stood a marble slab which supported a clear, ob-
long diamond with a black central core rimmed
green. Not unlike a giant eye, the stone winked
and shone with an intensity which further shattered the dream-Larson's confidence.

Silme stepped forward and presented a request
Larson could not hear in the frustratingly soundless world of his dream. The oracle passed a withered hand twice across the diamond. Mist swirled
in the depths of the gemstone, floated upward in
lines tenuous as heat haze. Abruptly the oracle
burst to a conflagration of yellow flame. Larson
reeled backward as a shapeless black form leaped
from the fire and attacked the startled sorceress.

Claws rent Silme's flesh. Blood sprayed the room
in arcs of red chaos. Gaelinar howled. His swords
reflected highlights of scarlet and gold. Valvitnir
rasped from its sheath. Larson and Gaelinar lunged
together for the demon which savaged Silme. The
beast's claws carved searing lines across Larson's

arm, but steel also met its mark. Valvitnir plunged deep into the monster's gut. Even more swiftly, Gaelinar's swords went sticky green with demon blood. It fell, witch-screaming, across Silme's lifeless form.

The room was awash with color. No life remained in Silme's broken body. The sapphire in her dragonstaff shattered like glass on the cold stone floor. Grief struck Larson in a wave of mental anguish. As he stared at the wild waste of multiple hues, the scene swirled and blurred away to a single black face with glowing red eyes. *Bramin!* Rationality escaped in a rush of fear, and sound sundered silence in a rolling thunderclap of evil laughter. Bramin's misshapen mouth formed words which struck like daggers of ice. "Be forewarned, *Al Larson*. Should you choose to seek the oracle, you will pay with the lives of friends!"

Bramin's face winked out. His dark hand remained and scattered the carefully placed barriers in Larson's mind. Memories burst forth like a torrent through a broken dam. Rockets flared from every angle with roars which deafened Larson. Bullets whined in insect-like swarms where he cowered with no safe place to retreat. Screams formed a chorus of hell-born agonies, while ghosts of buddies and enemies alike sentenced Larson to an eternity of life.

Larson's mental flight from madness ran him headlong into a scene from the past. He crouched between the banks of a dried river, clutching an M-16 which grew surprisingly light in the moments before death. Surrounded by enemies, he charged from the banks with Freyr's name on his lips. But where the last time he had recalled nothing except awakening in a strange elf body and a foreign world, now he recalled the torment of bullets riddling his body, jerking his limbs like a marionette. Horror held him screamless while a river of his own blood washed between the banks.

Larson awoke with sinews knotted and no sense of place or time. He was on his feet before he could think, eyes searching the room for movement. He scuttled to a corner and pressed his back to the wall. Sanity returned him to the blacksmith's cottage. Larson took several deep breaths, rose, and paced until his muscles uncoiled and his mood passed from panic to anxiety to crimson fury against the half-breed hellion who sought Silme's soul.

"Bramin!" Larson called with a courage he'd never before known he possessed. "I don't fear your threats, your dragons, your demons, or your . . ." Short of insults, he ended lamely, ". . . your piddling whangdoodles. Torment me as you wish, but we will visit this oracle. If you could kill Gaelinar or Silme, I think you would have done so already."

Larson believed his challenge was heard by no one except himself. But a shadow fell across the room, and the walls were suddenly suffused with a faint white glow. Caught in the center of the chamber, Larson spun like a fox between two packs of dogs. A message burned through his mind. "You underestimate me, Futurespawn." A long black finger probed his thoughts for a painful memory.

Prepared to fight though he saw no physical threat, Larson freed Valvitnir. Instantly, a benevolent entity joined the intruder in his mind. Bramin's mental presence hissed a shocked epithet and departed. Vidarr's reassurances pervaded

Larson's consciousness. Then the god, too, disappeared to Larson's perception.

Before the startled elf could ponder the significance of the night's events, Gaelinar poked his head through the door to Larson's chamber. "Practicing, hero? Good. You should be ready for your lesson."

After the sword practice, Larson found his stomach too knotted for food despite his twenty-four hour fast. The conversations of his companions passed unheard as Larson made the decision not to describe his dream to Silme. Too proud to reverse his decision about the oracle, he saw no reason to trouble the sorceress with Bramin's untenable threats. Still, time passed in an interminable vacuum; Larson was glad when he exchanged his final farewells and promises with Brendor. In bleary silence, he passed through the remainder of the town with Silme and Gaelinar and continued along the pine-bordered banks of the river Sylg.

The path looked distressingly similar to Larson's nightmare. Discomforted, he unsheathed Valvitnir and balanced the blade across his knees. His stilted replies to Silme's attempts at conversation frustrated the sorceress and earned him a lonely trip. Still, midday came far too soon for Larson. The sun hovered overhead when Silme drew up her mount at the road sign to the oracle of Hargatyr.

Gaelinar reined his mount and addressed Larson for the first time since his lesson. "You must be hungry. Sorry to go against your wishes not to pack supplies, but Lady Kelda offered fresh meat for our journey. I couldn't refuse. Gather some kindling, and we'll have the best cooked lunch of our wanderings."

Glad for any distraction which differentiated events of reality from those of his nightmare, Larson clambered from his saddle, sheathed his sword, and wandered into the woods. Twigs were plentiful on the forest floor. Larson selectively collected only the driest ones of reasonable length. A mere hundred yards from the crossroads, he had managed to accumulate a thick handful of kindling, and he started back toward his waiting companions.

Brush crackled behind Larson. He whirled, sticks scattering from his grip, in time to watch a small, familiar figure scuttle behind a clump of trees. "Brendor!" Larson screamed. He charged after the retreating child.

Brendor crashed awkwardly through the weeds. Slower, Larson trailed with far more stealth. Ragweed and ferns gave way to a brushless clearing enclosed by intertwining pine. Larson stopped, afraid the chase might already have taken him dangerously far from camp. "Brendor! Come out now! I know you're here, and I'm not playing games." He added with a gentle sigh, "I promise not to hit you."

The child's blunderings transformed to softer rustlings. Within moments, Brendor emerged from the brush and stepped among the shadows of the clearing. His clothing was torn. Small scratches beneath dripped blood. He shuffled toward Larson like a disobedient dog, his head bent low in shame, his eyes oddly vacant.

At a subtle noise from behind, Larson looked around to see Silme who had followed his calls to the edge of the clearing. He conveyed his control of the situation with a nearly imperceptible nod and returned his attention to the approaching child.

Less than an arm's length separated Larson and Brendor when Silme screamed, "Allerum, wait!" Enchantments bright as a flare struck the child and rebounded to glowing streamers. Silme's magics appeared to have no effect on the boy, but its backlash sparked light from a jagged blade clenched in his fist. Even as Larson recoiled in shock, Brendor plunged his knife at the elf's chest.

Reflexively, Larson caught the tiny wrist. Brendor's other hand enwrapped Larson's free forearm with a power he had never demonstrated in the past. The child's strength was awesome, despite his size. Larson strained until sweat sprang from his face. The dagger shivered ever closer.

"No!" A beam of amber screamed past Larson's ear and struck Brendor full in the face. Impact jerked the child backward. Desperate, Larson planted his foot on Brendor's knee and rolled onto his back. Stone bit into his spine. The child flipped over Larson, but his viselike grip held. Brendor's fingers pinned Larson's wrist to the ground. The dagger sped for the elf's bared throat. "Brendor, no!" Larson struggled like a madman. He seized Brendor's knife hand, but all his effort scarcely slowed the blade's descent.

Enchantments whizzed over Larson's head, plastering Brendor with multiple barbs of energy. The child flinched. Pain blanked his features as the magics ripped through his body and pitched him backward in a mass of bloody tatters. Larson heaved aside the limp figure and sprang to his feet, staring at the gruesome lump of flesh which was once a beloved companion. Brendor's eyes seemed glazed as marbles, and his blood-flecked hair spread in an inky puddle. Memory slapped Larson, heavy and unforgiving as a migraine. To Larson's mind, the clearing became a dirt road through a Vietnamese village; the bursts of sorcery transformed to the cruel blatter of an M-16.

The child's face was no longer Brendor's. The eyes slanted away from almond-colored irises. The mouth gaped, smeared with melted chocolate. *Ti Sun!* Larson's stomach lurched. His vision clouded to red haze. He turned hollow, accusing eyes on his buddy, Gavin, who still clutched his smoking gun. Profanities spilled from Larson's throat in an anguished sob. Blood fury raged like fever. He threw himself upon Gavin, swinging his fists with irrational, aimless outrage.

Many hands caught Larson. Men pinned him helplessly between uniformed bodies. Larson shrieked as he struggled. The fingers which bruised his arms caused a pain which only fueled his anger. Several seconds went by while Gavin carefully flipped Ti Sun's remains, and several more passed before Larson recognized the significance of the grenade which rolled from the child's limp hand. "It was him or you, you stupid bastard," Gavin explained with a wretched sob. "Him . . . or you."

The flashback broke to midday light. As Larson passed from one world to another, he discovered his fist poised to strike a figure already grounded by his blows. From nowhere, Gaelinar's hand seized his wrist and whipped his body to the ground with surprising speed. The Kensei's grip barred Larson's arm at an awkward angle. His other hand neatly caged Larson's throat. Larson knew Gaelinar could fracture arm or windpipe with a simple strike.

Larson lay perfectly still. His knuckles felt raw,

and his wrist was bruised from Brendor's attack. "I'm sorry," he whispered hoarsely.

Gaelinar's grip eased slightly. Silme knelt at Larson's side. Blood trickled from the side of her mouth, and Larson realized with a sudden rush of horror that she was the victim of his own crazed assault. "Oh my god. What have I done?"

Gaelinar released Larson. The elf staggered to his feet. He caught Silme in an embrace strengthened nearly to violence by the need for apology. "I'm sorry . . . I'm sorry . . ." Larson repeated it twenty times before humiliation broke his grip, and he turned away with self-loathing.

"Finish the quest without me." Larson unhooked Valvitnir and let the sword drop to the ground. "I could have killed her."

"I assure you, you couldn't have." Gaelinar drew to Larson's side. "Hero . . ."

"I'm not a hero!" Larson's screamed reply echoed between gangling pines and warped juniper. "I'm a raving lunatic, a madman, a paranoid maniac with delusions of . . . of . . . sanity . . ." When he ran out of Norse descriptions, he switched to English slang.

Gaelinar waited until the tirade passed and spoke with the sincerity he usually reserved for sword practice. "All heroes are flawed."

Larson whirled abruptly. "Heroes? Flawed?"

"All heroes," Gaelinar repeated. "To have courage, a man must know fear. Good cannot exist without evil. And a man becomes a hero when he excels despite his flaws."

Larson hesitated, mentally drained of emotion. Silme took his hands gently. "Hero, you are forgiven. I can't blame you for avenging the child, even against me. You couldn't know he was not the same Brendor we loved. Only my training as enchantress enabled me to recognize Bramin's influence when I reached the clearing."

"Then Brendor...?" Larson's voice quivered with hope.

Silme turned her gaze to her feet. "He's dead, Allerum. Bramin would need to destroy him completely to gain control of his body. I'm as sorry as you."

Larson hugged Silme again, grieved by the loss of a friend who was as a son and scarcely daring to believe the sorceress' unbounding compassion.

While Larson recovered his poise, Gaelinar set Brendor's body to pyre. It was only a formality. Bramin's automaton was a soulless shell no more worthy of dignity than a fallen sapling. Even so, Brendor's corpse left the world with a whispered eulogy and the Kensei's priceless respect.

As the three companions solemnly mounted horses and reined toward the oracle of Hargatyr, Larson confronted Gaelinar with a question. "Kensei, what's your flaw?"

Gaelinar's lips bent to a slight smile. "I, Lord Allerum, am no hero."

CHAPTER 6

Mageslayer

*"The haft of the arrow had been feath-
ered with one of the eagle's own plumes.
We often give our enemies the means of
our own destruction."*
—Aesop, The Eagle and the Arrow

The temple to Odin appeared far more benign in
reality than it had in Larson's dream. The ivy
which covered its walls was shaped and tended,
though cruel northern winds battered the vines
flatter on one side than the other. Age claimed its
toll in cracks, discolorations, and grime. Yet someone had taken the time to nurture bluebells at its
foundation, despite soil so solidly frozen it scarcely
supported the scraggly vegetables which were the
sustenance of oracle and acolytes.

Larson paced fretfully between Gaelinar and
Silme. The shock of Brendor's death had faded,
replaced by memories of the demon in his nightmare. Repeatedly, he replayed the scene in his
mind. Each time, the shapeless shadowform sprang
from the oracle's swirling mass of flame, shred-
ding Silme's body with talons sharp as steel. And

always Larson's defense came too late to save his beloved.

Silme knocked on the temple door. The heavy, wooden panel muffled sound nearly to silence. It was opened almost instantly by a young man who ushered Larson and his companions inside. He wore a clean gray cloak. Lines of hardship marred his features, but his lips curled in an amiable smile. He flicked away his hood, and hair the color of goldenrod fell to his shoulders. "Have you come to pay homage?"

Silme tapped the base of her dragonstaff against the earthen floor. "We wish to see the oracle."

The acolyte's expression grew grave. He led his new charges past groups of priests engaged in ritual. Light spilled through numerous windows, muted to gray haze by crudely thickset glass. Other acolytes nodded pleasantly as they passed, and Larson found nothing inherently threatening about the temple to Odin. Still, the memory of his nightmare wracked his spine with shivers, and anxiety closed him in an icy grip.

The acolyte led Larson and his companions past a row of three stone altars. The elf paused by the last, attracted by a stain dark as spilled wine. Closer inspection revealed the faint odor of death. Larson flinched back with a small cry and crashed against Gaelinar.

The Kensei turned swiftly and followed Larson's horrified gaze. He answered the unspoken question in a whisper. "War casualties, Allerum. Calm down. You've seen blood before." He caught the elf by a cloak sleeve and hauled him through a silver-threaded curtain identical to the one in the dream inspired by Bramin.

In the adjoining room, the oracle sat before her

marble table. As Larson, Silme, and Gaelinar stepped through the curtain, she raised her red-maned head. One blue eye examined her visitors with withering disdain. Beside it, a scarred socket gave mute testimony to the traumatic loss of her other eye. Leery of the oracle's disfigured and condemning features, Larson stared at the viewing stone before her. In the dream, he had thought the gemstone a diamond. Closer, he recognized it as a nearly transparent, oval-shaped block of quartz. Yet some work of nature or magic gave it the strange, eye-like configuration of green-irised black.

The oracle laced her long fingers on the table. Red hair streaked her knuckles like blood. "Welcome, Lady Silme, Sapphirerank." Her eye met Larson and Gaelinar in turn, but she extended them no greeting. "You have a question for my divination? Come forward."

Larson drew his sword and stepped forward with Silme. He poised a half stride before and to the right of the sorceress. His hand shook against Valvitnir's hilt. His tongue went dry as cotton. Hyperalert, Larson recognized Silme's drooping eyelids and shoulders and knew the enchantments she had channeled against Brendor had heavily tapped her physical energy.

The oracle's face went pale with a strange combination of anger and fear. "I'll not be threatened," she said softly. "There shall be no bare steel in my chamber."

Gaelinar gripped Larson's sword arm. "What's the matter with you?" he asked in a chastening whisper. "You've been acting strangely since we entered the temple."

Larson sheathed Valvitnir reluctantly. His reply was an anxious plea. "Just watch Silme. Please?"

Kensei Gaelinar scowled in offense, but he held his tongue with the subtlety of a master. "I always do," he answered after a moment. To Larson's relief, his instructor paced to Silme's other side.

The oracle waited until the men completed their exchange, then continued as if the disturbance had never occurred. "Your query, Dragonmage?"

Silme's words slurred slightly, as if the mere effort of gathering breath taxed her remaining strength. "Please, lady. My question concerns Allerum's sword, a quest, and the tranquillity of Midgard. Will hurling Valvitnir in the Helspring of Hvergelmir bring rescue or ruin to the gods of law and men?"

The oracle bent her head over the crystal, and her endless sea of hair covered the scrying stone like a curtain. Larson watched in horror as her wrinkled hand passed twice above the gemstone. He tried to loosen muscles coiled to pain by tension.

Silme yawned and rubbed fatigue from her eyes. Larson voiced a staccato grunt and edged closer to the sorceress. The oracle sat as still as death. Minutes dragged like hours. By the time the oracle looked up from her device, Larson had nervously worked his way directly in front of Silme.

The oracle's lips framed a smug smile which disappeared as she addressed Silme. "Have no fear, sorceress. Your quest is sanctioned. But quickly now; time runs short."

Silme looked around Larson with newfound energy, as if suddenly freed of some grave responsibility. "Thank you, lady. Your efforts may have saved our world from Chaos. May Odin continue to grace you with his favor."

"And Vidarr, you." The oracle returned the compliment in kind.

Irony made Silme wince. She turned, strode across the chamber, and passed through the shimmering curtain with Gaelinar at her heels. Larson retreated with more caution, gaze locked mistrustfully on the oracle whose lips pursed in antagonizing confidence. Wired, and eager to desert the red-haired seer who had become so abruptly lethal in his nightmare, Larson scrambled through the cloth slit. He jostled against Gaelinar in his haste.

The Kensei rolled his eyes with fading indulgence, and followed Silme around the milling acolytes. His glares grew less tolerant when Larson twice trod on his heels in his rush to vacate the temple to Odin. Once they stepped from the grayed interior of the building to the pleasure of afternoon, Larson loosed a shuddering sigh of relief. Even the biting winds seemed preferable to another moment of emotional agitation, especially to an elf impervious to winter's chill.

Larson and his companions mounted their horses. Ten minutes into their journey back toward the river Sylg, Larson shed the last of his apprehension and muttered to himself in triumph, "The half-breed ain't as all powerful as he thought."

Silme caught his arm. "Did you say something?"

Larson shook his head in denial. Then, seeing no reason to hide the truth from Silme any longer, he explained. "Bramin came to me in a dream and promised violence if we contacted the oracle. Idle threats, I'm certain, but just scary enough that I . . ." He broke off as Silme reined with an abruptness which sent her horse into a startled half rear.

"I thought I sensed his presence." Silme shaped her words with a self-accusatory anger. "But I blamed it on paranoia and weakness. Quickly now.

The oracle may be endangered." She turned her steed and kicked it to a gallop back toward Odin's temple.

Gaelinar whipped his horse about and reined after Silme. More accustomed to cars than horses, Larson clung to saddle and mane as his mount wheeled and followed its fellows at a run. They covered lost ground in minutes. Stopping only to tether the horses, Silme rushed to the dooryard, her companions close behind. Without troubling to knock, she pushed open the temple door. Priests looked up in alarm, but the sorceress paid them no heed. At a trot, she led Gaelinar and Larson through the slit in the silver-threaded curtain.

The oracle's chamber was as Larson remembered it from both dream and reality. Its dim, dank interior supported a marble block on which the eye-like crystal lay balanced on an edge. Gray cloth drapes covered the room's three walls. Conspicuously absent was the oracle of Hargatyr.

Larson waited by the slitted entrance, prepared for violence. Gaelinar stood in the center of the chamber, and his eyes followed Silme's anxious path. The sorceress peered behind the marble, paused a moment in confusion, then trotted to a far corner. She peeled aside a corner of the curtain which hid the back wall. Matched, gold-tasseled cords fell into her hand. When she pulled one, the cloth parted. Beyond, Larson and his companions saw a smaller chamber.

Gaelinar strode around Silme and entered the room first. Larson crossed the scrying chamber in time to step around the curtain with Silme. Behind a writing desk and before a simple cot, a pallid body sprawled, face downward, on the floor.

Red hair spread about the narrow shoulders and waist in a mass of tangles.

"No," said Silme softly.

Gaelinar eased the corpse to its back. The oracle's single eye was closed tight beside the massively scarred empty socket. Her breasts, thighs, and torso were violet with pooled blood. Though more familiar with rapid decomposition in the heat of Vietnam, Larson knew the oracle had been dead for several hours at least. The thought left him with a head-pounding certainty. *The woman who had answered Silme's question and sanctioned their quest was not the oracle of Hargatyr.*

Gaelinar ushered his grieving companions back into the scrying room and pulled the curtain closed, leaving the oracle what little decency remained in death. Silme pressed her back to the marble table, laid her staff at her feet, and buried her face in her palms. Exhaustion from wasted enchantments and frustration preyed heavily on her remaining strength. She looked as vulnerable as a child.

Larson lowered himself beside Silme and rested his arm across her sagging shoulders. "What now?"

Silme sighed. "All I dare believe of the false oracle's prophecy is the value of time. We still don't know how to free Vidarr. I'm certain only that we mustn't surrender him to the Helspring." She fell silent and still. Just as Larson convinced himself she had fallen asleep, she rallied internal energy and leaped to her feet.

Silme knocked Larson aside and paced with the steady tred of a caged tiger. "If Fates or gods know the method of breaking Loki's spell, the answer lies in the stone of Hargatyr." She indicated the crystal. "Anyone who understands its enchantments can tap its knowledge."

"And you?" asked Larson hopefully.

Silme paused, hands against the marble. She shook her head. "Dragonrank magic taps its caster's life energy. That's what makes it so powerful and desirable, and also dangerous. Devices like the gemstone are of no more use to me than crossbow bolts to a longbowman. I have the basic knowledge, but too many gaps exist to correctly glean information."

"Try, at least." Larson rose.

Silme caught his hands. Her palms left sweaty prints on the edge of the marble table. "I can do better than try. Another in this room may have some of the knowledge I need. Allerum, did Vidarr tell you why he can communicate only with you?"

Larson tried to recall. "He said people from my world lack mind barriers."

Silme dropped his hands, eyes widening incredulously. "None?"

Larson shrugged. "I suppose. I don't even know what it means."

"For now, it means a way to link myself with Vidarr." Silme's gaze dropped to the sword at Larson's hip. "Together, we may fathom the workings of the oracle's stone." Her cheeks colored slightly, but she continued eagerly. "Allerum, can you hold your mind blank?"

"My mind? Blank? No!" He flinched back as the sorceress' request became clear. The thought that Silme might access his memories of murder made him light-headed. "My mind runs and lapses without my control. From moment to moment, I don't know if I'll find myself here or home, whether I'm experiencing reality, memory, or the inspired illusions of trapped gods and vicious warlocks. For me, Silme, blank is not a state of mind."

Larson had quite forgotten Gaelinar stood behind him. The Kensei's husky voice made him
jump. "It is now, hero. Would you have us damn
the world for your reluctance?"

Silme finished the appeal more gently. "I re-
quire only that you keep people and places from
your consciousness. Concentrate on naming foods
or counting twigs, anything repetitive which requires channeling thought. Will you try it?"

"I've no choice." Larson swallowed around a
lump which grew in his throat. "What do I have to
do?"

"Sit." Silme waved him to the floor.

Larson sat, knees pressed to his chest. His hands
trembled as he watched Silme reach for the crystal
of Hargatyr. "Wait!"

Silme paused.

"How do you know Bramin hasn't tampered
with the stone or replaced it with something evil?"

Silme seized the eye-like gem with an impatient
toss of her head. "This is Odin's temple. The
oracle's scrying stone must be warded by Law. A
simple touch would maim or even kill Bramin. It
would reflect his destructive magics. Any other
attempt to remove it from the temple would re-
quire him to work it past a room full of priests."
Silme lowered herself to the floor before Larson
and placed the stone between them. "Lay the sword
across your legs."

Larson complied reluctantly. Valvitnir buzzed
slightly against him, glowing with blue light. "Silme.
Shouldn't we wait until you've had some rest."

Silme locked her fingers between Larson's. Her
voice became a low drone. "No time. Bramin can
trace us through the gaps in your mind. We don't
want him to know we discovered his treachery."

Silme let her eyes fall shut. Her head lolled forward.

"Silme?"

"What!" Impatience made her curt.

"What if I can't control my thoughts?"

Her voice assumed a hiss of dry warning. "Let's just hope you can."

Her reply did nothing to reassure Larson. Near panic, he chose to conjugate verbs from his high school French lessons. *Je suis, tu es, il est. . . .* Twin presences pressed against his mind with the banding grip of a headache. Vidarr and Silme scuttled without direction, silent as mice in the jarring loops of Larson's flawed thought pattern. God and sorceress probed blindly for one another, and Larson felt all too aware of their locations.

Nous sommes, vous etes, ils . . . ils sont. . . . Gradually, Silme and Vidarr closed the distance between their mental presences. Their union broke to a dazzling explosion of light, sparking one of Larson's frayed memories like a dried piece of kindling. Hurled into flashback, Larson stared at a mine crater the size of his bedroom back in the States. Then a barrier snapped into place with a force which broke the illusion. Threat carved into focus. *Hold your thoughts! I've no power to rescue you again.*

J'ai, tu as, il a, nous avons. . . . Larson plunged into his studies with desperate passion. The combined essence of Vidarr and Silme wove drunkenly through his brain. A flurry of enchantments battered through consciousness unsteady as fever. *VOUS AVEZ. . . . Will hurling Valvitnir in the Hel spring of Hvergelmir bring rescue or ruin to the gods of law and men?* Silme's question echoed through

Larson's mind, pulling him from his furious attempts at conjugations.

Smoke eddied like car exhaust. The fused presence gasped in triumph, then hissed in fury as the haze peeled away, like scalded wax, without answer. *Je vais, tu.* . . . Frustration settled in Larson's mind, dimmed to resolution. Silme/Vidarr gathered energy, unwittingly tapping him in the process.

Reference folded in nightmare as magics enwrapped him in drugged awareness. Fog thick as earth warped vision. Another alien presence winked to life in Larson's already overcrowded mind. *Destroying the sword heralds Vidarr's death. Beware! Such an action will doom the world to Chaos.*

Sanity flickered. *Tu vas, il va, nous allons, vous allez, ils allont!* Emotion pervaded him in a perfect mixture of outrage and concern. Silme/Vidarr coiled like a cat prepared to spring. Magic formed a tense ball in Larson's mind, crushing aside fragile circuits of memory. Pain blurred thought to blackness. *Je fais, tu fais, il fait.* . . . Rationality exploded to madness.

A painted forest replaced the emptiness of Larson's eye-closed world. He walked between Silme and Vidarr beneath a mercilessly hot sun. Blue haze ringed the sorceress, and the god shone with a golden glory. *Where the hell?* thought Larson. *Oh . . . a . . . nous faisons.* The syllables warped to nonsense. Suddenly, a woman tall as a watchtower stepped from the brush, directly in his path.

Larson recoiled. The life auras of god and sorceress fused to glaring green. "Who are you?" demanded Silme boldly.

"I am Skuld, *Future.*" The giantess' voice rattled trees. "In what cause have you summoned me, Silme Sapphirerank?"

"The cause of men and gods." Silme replied
nearly as loud. "Should Chaos claim this world,
there shall be no Law nor time nor knowledge.
You and your sister Fates would perish." Her entreaty rolled like thunder through the silence of
the forest. "How must we free Vidarr from imprisonment?"

A breeze rose and fell, rose and fell again. Several seconds passed before Larson recognized the
wind as the breath of the giantess Skuld. "Your
fears are founded, Lady Silme. Your quest is hon-
orable, though it brings doom upon others, men
and women of my domain, those ruled by one of
your companions and beloved by the other. It is
not my place to judge your task nor prevent it.
The answer to your question lies with my sisters."
Skuld marched back into the forest, trampling
trees like matchsticks.

The giantess' prophecy sounded strange to Larson's numbed mind. *How could rescuing men from
Chaos doom them for the future?* Before he found
time to ponder the question, another woman shouldered between the trees. She looked sufficiently
like Skuld to be her sister, yet not similar enough
to be a twin.

"I am Verdandi," the giantess said, though no
one asked her name. "I hold title to the present.
Your query has gone beyond my realm to the
past. I can tell you only that your quest stands
contested by a god and a half-breed with the power
to destroy you." Swiftly, she returned to the forest.

Cold sweat ran down Larson's back, and he
shook with chills despite the heat. The third sister
of Fate glided from the tangled brush. Vertigo
transformed her to a blur which sharpened slowly
to detail. She was obviously the eldest of the

giantesses, smaller, withered, face puckered with burdens transferred from her sisters by time.

"I am Urdr, keeper of the past and the understanding of Odin. It was I who added the final provision to Loki's spell, and I who shall reveal that knowledge to you. To free my lord, Vidarr, the elf must claim Loki's life with the blade Valvitnir."

Shock battered Larson, obscured Urdr in glare. Silme's scream pierced his mind like a spear, jarring loose a wild memory. The sound transformed to the shrill whine of jets. Even as Larson located the blood-red afterburners of the paired phantoms, he recognized his surroundings. He traveled a familiar road in the Mekong Delta. Some distance ahead, a dozen buddies in cammie paused in horror as they discovered the jets' target was the same village which had, moments before, been their destination.

The lead jet passed over the village. A raging column of flame consumed grass huts and villagers without mercy. Panicked screams made Larson cringe. Even as the gasoline fumes pinched his nose, he realized he was neither in flashback nor alone. The dry crackle of gathering magics made him whirl toward Silme and Vidarr. "Oh my god! Silme, no!"

His warning came too late. Sorceries howled past his ear with all the inhuman speed of the phantoms. Bluish magics impacted the trailing jet and broke to a savage explosion of emerald. Shards of twisted steel rained to earth. Larson's sinews went taut with shock. He could only suppose Silme saw the jets as dragons swooping upon an innocent town. Ahead on the road, the camouflaged men dropped, as one, to the ground. Suddenly,

Larson knew he and his otherworld companions had become the enemy.

"Down!" hollered Larson. He dove into the roadside ditch. Gunfire popped and sputtered around him, sounding oddly impotent after the scourge of napalm and the thunderclap of Silme's spell. With no means or desire to return fire on his buddies, Larson flattened to the dirt without recourse. *What have I done?* Worried over the ignorance of his alien companions, he forced his gaze toward the road. Vidarr and Silme stood behind a shimmering curtain which reflected bullets like a wall.

The oddity of their magical defense was not lost on the Americans. One yelled. "Holy fucking god!" Silme began a new incantation. Dark mists broiled from her fingertips. A graying glow flickered around the enchantress and winked out like a spent candle. As Silme drained her life energy, she fell in a soundless faint.

"Silme!" screamed Larson. The sorceress lay still within her magical shield, but her final spell was cast, Wizardry rolled along the road like a living ball of fire. The men in cammie dodged from the path of the sorceries with startled cries. And, from over the burning village, Larson caught sight of the returning phantom. Faster than its own report, the jet glided toward them in vengeful silence.

"No!" Larson hollered. Smoke from the smoldering village swirled like ghosts into the phantom's twin intakes. Larson lay frozen in terror. A rocket dropped from beneath the jet, plummeted, then shot forward with a speed which outdistanced the plane. Before Larson could scream, the missile crashed to ground with a blast of red-orange. Its explosion seemed to shatter earth. Though the magical shield contained most of its impact, force crashed against Larson's head and knocked him to oblivion.

Larson awakened to utter darkness. Screams of terror ripped from his lungs and reverberated like distant answers. Throat raw, he fell to silence and recognized the slosh of running water. The rasp of a sword scraping from its sheath restored his rationality. Larson struggled to legs stiff with disuse. His hand closed about Valvitnir's hilt. "Gaelinar?" he whispered hopefully.

Gaelinar's gruff reply had never seemed so welcome. "I should have known it was you, hero. How do you feel?"

"Shaky," Larson admitted. "And blind." A scene threaded through his mind, the memory of Silme lying still as death on a road in the Mekong Delta. "Where's Silme?"

The sorceress called over the bubbling of the river Sylg. "Here. The real question, Allerum, is where *was* Silme."

Larson groped toward Silme's voice. "My world. I'm sorry. I tried to control my memories, I swear I did, but . . ." Silme caught his arm. It occurred to Larson with frightening abruptness that the surrounding darkness was too complete for night. He finished with an anxious whine. "Dammit, why can't I see?"

Gaelinar replied. "We're in the Valley of Darkness."

"H-how?"

"We carried you," Silme explained. "Bramin can only track us through your mind. With you unconscious, we traveled as quickly as we could."

Larson pulled Silme closer. "Why are we still headed toward Hvergelmir?"

Gaelinar sounded nearer. "Because Loki expects us there. He wants your sword destroyed in the Helspring, and for all he knows we plan to complete that quest. He'll be there to make certain it gets done."

"Please, Allerum" Silme spoke with concern. "Talk with Vidarr. Make certain he's all right after . . . what happened."

Reluctantly, Larson released Silme and drew Valvitnir. The sword quivered mournfully in his grip. Vidarr's mental presence wound cautiously through the fragile tangles of his mind. *I pity your people. The men of your world removed all the glory from war and left only killing.*

Larson jammed the sword into its sheath and broke his link with Vidarr. "He's fine," Larson grumbled. But the god's assessment echoed through his mind, awakening a terrifying thought. *When we complete this quest and the gods of Asgard no longer need me, what becomes of me? Will Freyr return me to the skill-less death machine of the Vietnam war?*

With a strength born of imagined injustice, he jerked the sword free again. *Vidarr. . . ?*

The god answered defensively before Larson finished the question. *I don't know what Freyr plans! My own fate is tenuous enough. Since my imprisonment, I know only what I see through your eyes.*

Damn! Larson dashed the sword to the ground. Its blue flare faded darkness in a circle of purple. Larson crushed Silme to his chest in frustration, and her dragonstaff cracked painfully against his shoulder. His lips brushed her face, found her mouth, and pressed into a passionate kiss. Desire burned him like fire, but he loosened his grip and fought bitterness. "Silme, the success of this quest may doom us to separate worlds." Grief caught the words in his throat. "There is a link between our worlds, even if it's only in my mind. We passed through it once. I swear, if Freyr sends me back to Nam, I'll find a way to return to you."

Larson heard the scrape of metal against sand as Silme hefted Valvitnir and returned the sword to its sheath. "Or if necessary, I'll find you," she told him gently. "It's not often I meet a hero like you."

Gaelinar shuffled his feet, and sand showered against Larson's ankles. "Forgive me. If we don't move along soon, we forfeit whatever advantage we gained. Allerum?"

Larson felt a slight breeze of movement. A ration sack thumped into his side. He accepted the pouch and slung it across his shoulder. "Where are the horses?"

"They refused to enter the valley." Gaelinar's voice came from some distance ahead. "Animals can sense evil."

Larson caught Silme's hand and trotted after the Kensei. Two days had passed since his last meal, but Larson felt no hunger. His stomach balled in an aching knot of tension. Soon he would face the greatest challenge of any life. He would become a godslayer or damn his soul and Silme's to an eternity of torture.

A victim of his own doubts, Larson did not notice as darkness diffused to gray. But another in the party was more wary. Gaelinar stopped, silent in the mist, and caught his companions as they passed. "Caution," he warned. "We're approaching the Helspring. I hear the falling waters."

Larson released Silme's hand and wiped slick

palms on his cape. Beyond the gurglings of the
river Sylg, Larson heard a sound like a roomful of
serpents. The air felt suddenly chill. For the first
time since his recovery, Larson discerned huddled
cliffs which hemmed the Valley of Darkness. The
river Sylg spanned nearly four times its earlier
width, and ice blocks as large as a man's head
bobbed in its current.

Gaelinar drew his katana and tested its edge
with his thumbnail. "Ready?"

"Ready?" repeated Larson incredulously. "Ready!
Loki's a god. Shouldn't we make a plan of some
sort?" His own words struck with mind-jarring
force. *We're fighting a god. Like Christ or something.
What chance do we have?*

Gaelinar sheathed the katana, trading it for his
companion sword. His hand slid along the blade,
but Larson could not perceive the Kensei's expression in the semidarkness. "I cut him. Silme throws
spells. And you . . ." Gaelinar paused thoughtfully,
". . . bested the guard captain of Forste-Mar before
your first sword lesson. So, I guess you hit people,
too."

Larson paced to hide his trembling hands. "Loki's
not people. He's a . . . a god."

Gaelinar walked toward the palisades, and his
figure was lost to the hovering shadows of the
Valley of Darkness. "He can die just like we can."

Silme caught for Larson's arm, but her hand
slipped free in the sweat which slicked his limbs
like grease. "Loki's both a wizard and a swordsman, which gives him a large repertoire for attack. Plans become worthless against a god as
unpredictable as his Chaos, especially when one of
the parties privy to the strategy can't hide his
knowledge from the enemy."

Larson nodded his understanding. Silme and Gaelinar might have plotted while he recovered from the phantom's rocket, but anything they told him could become accessible to Loki through the flaws in his mind. Doubt rushed down upon Larson, merciless as a volley of gunfire. "I'm not prepared to war with gods. I may never be." *A private in one of the bloodiest wars in history, and I've never even killed a man with my own hands. The murders on my conscience were all the impersonal and distant victims of an M-16.* Yet the gun he had wielded lay without guilt between the banks of a dried river in a body-littered jungle, while the screams of the dying haunted the memory of Al Larson. Larson stopped pacing and deliberately avoided touching Valvitnir.

"Allerum!" Threat colored Gaelinar's words. "Freyr brought you to complete this quest at a price a mere mortal cannot comprehend. You will fight gods, I promise. Need I remind you there are three gods of Chaos and fifteen of Law? Choose your enemies with care."

Larson fixed on the first numerical fact. "*Three* gods!" he screamed, nearly hysterical.

Silme clarified quickly. "Loki's daughter, Hel, can't cross the bridge from her citadel. As for Helblindi . . ."

"He's trapped in a sword, too," Larson interrupted as he recalled Vidarr's vision. "Loki's sword." His hand dropped unconsciously to Valvitnir.

Vidarr's mental presence filled his mind like storm wind. *Bramin's sword,* he corrected. *And you should know something. Freyr brought you here with full knowledge that the choice to face Loki must remain your own. I want freedom, but it's your right to know the gods of Law are not vindictive. Slay Loki or not as your conscience sanctions. A moral decision will not be held against you.* Vidarr ended contact with Larson, though not quickly enough to hide the grief which lapped Larson's mind like a tide.

"Ready," said Larson softly. Resolved, he filled his lungs with air and exhaled through clenched teeth. "Let's go."

Silme followed Larson through the lightening mists of the valley. The cliffs ended abruptly. The river washed across a plain of dying grasses, then plummeted through a pit as large as a mine crater. Larson strode from the valley; wind bitter as hoarfrost whipped hair into his eyes. Anyone but a native to the climate would have found it unbearably cold, but as a creature of faery, Larson was impervious. The rapid change from darkness to daylight made him blink, though clouds obscured the sun with gloom.

Larson's eyes adjusted quickly. He recognized ten similar valleys radiating from the central chasm like the spokes of a giant wheel. Curious, he trotted forward; weeds crushed to powder beneath his feet. The rush of waters through the pit grew loud as a lion's roar, and then faded as Larson's ears adjusted to the noise. As he neared the edge of the cliff, he found a narrow path which threaded into the abyss. Poised at its lip, he saw a sight more breathtaking than the falls of Niagara.

Eleven rivers plunged as one through the rounded crater, their waters wound in a shimmering braid. The pittance of light which pierced the clouds drew glittering lines through the torrent crashing into the Helspring. Droplets bounced upward in a frozen mist and pelted Larson's face like hail. Entranced, he took a step forward. A stone broke loose beneath his foot. He went giddy as he imagined himself tumbling with it, weaving through the cascade, smashed to lifeless, soulless waste beneath Hvergelmir's current.

A shiver traversed Larson. He shielded his eyes and shied away just as Silme bellowed. "Loki!" Her voice echoed about the many valleys. "We know you're here. If you want Valvitnir in Hvergelmir, come get him."

Larson whirled and freed his sword, edging nervously from the Helspring. Gaelinar waited near the valley. Silme stood, ready, in the center of the plain. Her challenge went unanswered.

"Loki!" Silme started again.

Bramin glided from the waning fog of Sylg's valley, black as oblivion. The winds of the waterfalls swirled iron gray robes about his torso. His eyes flashed red threat from shadowed sockets. The diamond in his staff glowed bright as a street lamp. "Did you think Loki would waste energy on you?" As he spoke, a sunburst of sorceries blossomed in his hand. "You're scarcely worth my time."

Gaelinar moved first. Fast as thought, his fingers freed a shuriken. Even as he tensed his arm to throw, Bramin's enchantments sheeted through the air. A raw blaze of magic enwrapped the Kensei in a glimmering net which held him still as stone.

"No!" screamed Silme. Light pulsed across the plain as wizard and sorceress howled spell words forceful as explosions. Bramin's diamond blazed through a chaotic spectrum of color. His raging red eyes locked suddenly on Larson, and Silme loosed a short scream. Her tone changed abruptly. A beam of ruddy light leaped from Bramin's fingers. Silme's magical parry pinwheeled protectively before Larson.

Bramin cursed, then laughed as his spell shattered to colored highlights. Sunbright sorceries surrounded both Dragonrank mages in a wave which blinded Larson. Light blazed and died; magics fizzled. Silme dropped to her knees as Larson lunged at Bramin. Valvitnir arced over Larson's head and sliced toward the half-breed.

In a single motion, Bramin dropped his staff, drew his sword and blocked. Six inches of air separated the swords when they stopped abruptly. The motion jarred both wielders. The half-breed riposted. Larson jerked his blade upward in instinctive defense. Bramin's sword shied awkwardly from Valvitnir, as if of its own accord.

Larson and Bramin recovered together. In the brief respite, Vidarr's presence imparted a panicked message. *Helblindi and I are prisoners of the same spell. A touch will destroy us both!*

Conditioned, Larson repeated the first maneuver Gaelinar had taught him. Valvitnir whistled reluctantly around him and lanced toward Bramin. Bramin sprang forward as he blocked. The swords quivered, desperate inches apart. Too close for an adequate sweep, the half-breed retreated.

Drop me, damn you! Vidarr's command pierced Larson's mind with painful force.

Larson responded with a desperate thought. *Drop you and die! I can't face Bramin weaponless!*

Bramin thrust. Larson waved Valvitnir before his body, and Helblindi sprang aside. Bramin swung low. Larson withdrew his front foot, but the Helblade scraped skin from his calf.

Larson swore, deaf to Vidarr's pleas. Again, he sprang at Bramin and skipped back as the half-breed returned his strike. Apology rolled through his mind in waves. Vidarr gathered mental strength, dragged Larson's consciousness with him in a short conspiracy with Helblindi.

Larson's breath came in wild sobs. He repositioned his sword, just in time to block a sweep for his neck. Vidarr tore free of his grip and tumbled through the air like a wounded bird. To Larson's relief, Helblindi also pitched from its wielder's hand.

Bramin paused a moment in shock, then retreated across the plain. Larson noticed the sharp sting of ice pellets on the back of his neck, and only just realized how close Bramin had maneuvered him to a fatal plunge into the Helspring. Cautiously, he came forward to face the sorcerer in the dying grasses. Over Bramin's wide, black shoulders, he saw Silme watching with wide-eyed helplessness. She mouthed a silent message: I love you. Beyond her, Gaelinar stood motionless as a painting.

Bramin lashed, backhanded, at Larson's face. The elf blocked with his left arm. Before he could return the strike, Bramin closed. The half-breed's foot kicked painfully against the back of Larson's knee, and his elbow crashed against Larson's chin. Larson staggered, recovered. As Bramin realigned, Larson sprang and punched. Bramin blocked effortlessly. His dark fist smashed Larson's nose.

Larson lurched as sparks danced before his eyes. Dizzied with nausea, he tried to think. Bramin's maneuvers came with practiced speed and machinelike efficiency. Larson knew he could never avoid the blows. He could only hope to endure.

Resolved, he jabbed at Bramin's face. Again, the half-breed blocked and returned the strike. This time, Larson took the punch. Pain exploded across his jaw, but he bore in on his enemy. His knee

crashed into Bramin's groin. The half-breed gasped.
Silme screamed. Larson's elbow thrust toward
Bramin's head. The half-elf ducked, using Lar-
son's own momentum to hurl him to the ground.
Bramin's foot lashed out, passing over Larson's
head as the elf rolled to his feet.

Several yards away, Silme rolled in the grass as
if in pain. Bramin's features twisted in a savage
smile. His hands rested peacefully at his sides as
he raised his face to Larson. "Go ahead, hero." He
spat the last word in contempt. "Hit me."

Larson did not need prompting. Bramin made
no attempt at defense. Larson's fist smashed into
his face, and Silme shrieked in agony. Stunned,
Larson did not press his advantage.

Blood trickled from Bramin's nose, but his mouth
parted in silent laughter. "Hit me again, elf cow-
ard." Malice danced in his feral eyes. "Hurt Silme!"

With a cry of anger, Larson struck. Cartilage
snapped beneath his knuckles, jarring Bramin to
his knees. Silme howled in torment. Her body
writhed in the dirt.

Alarmed, Larson started toward her. "Silme?"
As Bramin rose and advanced, Larson turned back
to the fight. "What have you done to her?" he
demanded. Hysteria raised his voice an octave.

Blood colored Bramin's mouth scarlet. "I did
nothing," he replied triumphantly. He flicked blood
from his cheek. "But every time you mar this pretty
face, you injure hers as well."

Larson retreated defensively, afraid to strike.
Bramin swept forward. His left foot drove into
Larson's gut with a force which doubled him over.
As Bramin completed his spin, his right foot jolted
against Larson's head. Larson rolled clumsily, await-
ing a death stroke which never fell. Confidence

made Bramin patient as a cat. He explained while
Larson struggled dizzily to his feet. "To save you
from my sorceries, Silme linked her life aura to
mine. She holds our magic inoperative, but our
souls are fused. Her fate and mine have become
one."

Bramin faked a foot strike. As Larson dodged,
Bramin delivered a brazenly high kick. His heel
slammed against Larson's forehead. Impact snapped Larson's neck rearward. The back side of his
skull struck the ground first. Darkness swam down
on him. Larson shook his throbbing head, watching Bramin's retreating back through a veil of
colored mist.

Fury gave Larson renewed strength. He charged
Bramin's back, just as the sorcerer bent for his
Helsword. Larson punched. Bramin wheeled. His
elbow caught Larson in the gut. The half-breed
seized Larson's outstretched arm and hurled the
elf over his shoulder.

Accustomed to wrestling, Larson struck the
ground, unhurt. Bramin knelt beside him, pin-
ning his right wrist to the ground. Larson rocked
toward the half-breed, wrapped his left arm about
one dark leg, and rolled. Bramin flipped to the
ground. Even as he landed, Larson reversed direction. The force pitched Bramin to his stomach,
hands trapped beneath his chest. Larson pressed
his full weight against the half-breed. His one
hand clutched a swarthy wrist. His forearm thrust
Bramin's face in the dirt.

Silme screamed between panting gasps. "Kill him,
Allerum! Forget me. Kill him!"

Larson jolted his fist against the back of Bramin's
skull, cursing himself for Silme's pained whimper.
He released Bramin and seized Helblindi's hilt

before the half-breed could do anything more than roll to his back. Larson spun and pressed the blade to Bramin's throat. The sorcerer went still. His face drained of color; his chest heaved. "If you kill me, you kill Silme, too." Bramin warned in a reedy whine.

Larson's hand shook. Sick with worry, he called over his shoulder. "*Is it true?*"

Silme made no reply.

Larson twisted toward the sorceress. "Damn you, is it true?"

"Yes," she whispered. "It's true, but . . ."

Bramin clawed to his feet and ran. Gaelinar's training resurfaced mechanically. Larson struck. Helblindi's blade carved through Bramin's hamstring. The muscle curled into a ball. Bramin collapsed. Larson finished the strike from habit gained from hours of practice. He thrust the blade through Bramin's chest. The half-breed quivered, then fell limp, and Silme's dying scream reverberated in accusation.

Anguish tore denial from Larson's throat. "No! No!" He ripped Helblindi free and cast it aside in wild sorrow. Blood splashed as the blade tumbled awkwardly to the ground, and Larson fell with it. Grief-mad, he howled like a wounded animal and crawled to Silme's prone form. She lay like a marble carving beside the blade which imprisoned her god. Larson dropped to her side. She was cold as ice and every bit as still. Tears burned his eyes like poison, cleaning tracks through the blood which stained his chin. His gaze fell upon the motionless Kensei, and he howled anguished curses at the swordmaster who had drilled him until the sword figure which killed Silme became reflex.

Larson's sanity crumbled to a muddle of thought.

His fist struck the ground with a force which jarred his arm to the shoulder. His second blow landed against Valvitnir's blade; its sharpened edge slit the side of his hand. Oblivious to physical pain, Larson caught the sword by its hilt. Vidarr filled his mind with warning. *Allerum, behind you!*

CHAPTER 7

Godslayer

*"Death closes all: but something ere the end,
Some work of noble note, may yet be done,
Not unbecoming men that strove with gods."*
—Alfred Lord Tennyson, Ulysses

Larson whirled. Light lanced toward him from the direction of the valleys. He cringed defensively. The magics struck Valvitnir and broke to streamers vivid as rockets. "Yow!" Larson dropped flat to the ground. The valleys seemed to mock him, black as moonless night, yet somewhere in the gloom stalked a sorcerer more dangerous than any sniper. *Is it Loki?*

Yes, Vidarr confirmed. *Look up. And lift your sword, or I won't be able to shield you from his spells*

Pressed tight to the dirt out of habit, Larson raised his eyes. Reddish light hovered on a crag above Sylg's valley. In its center, Loki gestured, menacing as a demon in a fire pit. His sorceries streaked toward Larson with a roar like thunder. Larson rolled aside. Enchantments swirled into a

fizzling whirlwind and funneled into Valvitnir's
blade. *How?*

Vidarr's presence seemed weak in Larson's mind.
*Not certain. Some aspect of Loki's imprisonment spell
renders me capable of negating his other magics.* Vidarr's
reply came, labored as a winded asthmatic. *But it
requires concentration. . . .*

Larson rose to a crouch, seeking cover. On the
cliff face, light flared around Loki, brief and glorious as a dying star. Larson squinted against its
brilliance. Red and green shadows winked on the
inside of his eyelids. When he recovered his vision, Loki was gone.

Where is he? Dammit, where is he? Larson spun like
a dancer, sword pressed to his chest in a position
more appropriate for a gun.

Be still! Vidarr chastised, but his tone betrayed
fear.

Between Sylg's valley and Larson, sorceries
blazed. He raised Valvitnir offensively, shielding
his eyes as light billowed to agonizing intensity, a
mocking column of white flame. The enchantments broke suddenly to traces. Ahead, Loki appeared, sword readied, beneath his fading magics.

Larson felt Vidarr poised to fight enchantments.
Loki lunged forward. Larson blocked. The blades
met in a shower of glittering sparks. Impact jarred
Larson to the elbow. He staggered backward, re-
covering just in time to block a second strike. The
force of Loki's blow drove Larson nearly to his
knees.

Loki's assault seemed ceaseless. His strokes came
fast and were rhythmically competent. They left
Larson no opening for anything but awkward blocks
and retreat. The god's face pinched in concentration. Yet, despite Larson's obvious inexperience,

Loki treated his opponent like a worthy threat. He displayed none of Bramin's assuredness. Loki knew overconfidence contrives incompetence.

Larson defended as well as he could, but his efforts seemed woefully inadequate. Loki's sword bit rents in his tunic and skin. Any one of the god's maneuvers could easily have taken Larson's life. But Loki's strategy soon became obvious. He would drive wielder and godsword into the Helspring together, obviating the need to handle Valvitnir himself. And Larson was helpless to prevent him.

Loki's sword wove a wall of steel, herding Larson toward Hvergelmir as a shepherd does an errant sheep. The sharp nicks of his enemy's blade reawakened the throbbing pains left from Larson's fight with Bramin. Tortured sinews screamed with every movement. His face felt as if it were on fire. He tried to stand firm against Loki's hammering blows, but his body could no longer obey.

Blow after blow rang against Valvitnir. Larson's ears buzzed, then roared. Ice shards prickled the back of his neck. The cold made him realize, with sudden terror, that the noises in his head did not come from within; Loki had driven him to the verge of Hvergelmir's pit.

"Christ!" Larson dredged deep for reserves of energy. Strength flowed back into his limbs. But the effort of blocking Loki's strokes drained his second wind almost instantly. Fatigue obscured Larson's vision to a blur. Sweat stung the many scratches inflicted by Loki. Scarcely able to lift his arms, Larson could only retreat and let Valvitnir tend defense.

Loki bore in. Larson recoiled. The ground fell out beneath his heel. Near panic, he staggered away from the ledge and nearly impaled himself on Loki's blade. Hope shattered beneath a wild explosion of despair. *What the hell am I fighting for anyway?*

Vidarr's reply seemed weak, as if the efforts of defense cost him as much as Larson. *Loved ones, Allerum. The future, my freedom . . .*

And liberty and justice for all. . . .

Loki's eyes glittered, violet-blue as gemstones. He drew back his arm for the final lunge.

Loved ones, Vidarr? Larson's thoughts grew bitter. *Silme's dead. She's dead by my own hand. Silme is DEAD! Whose cause . . .*

Vidarr jerked upward to block. *Her cause! And the cause of all men in the future.*

Larson stood, ready to accept the death promised by Loki's descending sword. *The Fate giantess, Skuld, claimed freeing you would doom my people.*

Vidarr's mental presence went oddly silent. Loki lanced forward.

Larson demanded an answer. *Vidarr!*

Gaelinar! Vidarr's cry echoed through Larson's consciousness. Hope displaced futility in a corner of his mind. A shuriken skimmed through the air, visible only as a glint from a sun ray. It embedded in Loki's sword hand with a nearly inaudible thunk.

Loki uttered a startled oath. Rather than drop his sword, he pulled his thrust. Holding his blade between Larson and himself, Loki twisted toward his new antagonist. Magics crackled from his outstretched left hand and sheeted toward Kensei Gaelinar.

"No!" Concerned for Gaelinar's life, Larson struck. His upstroke crashed into Loki's armpit, and bit through muscle. Loki screamed. The shuriken dislodged from his hand, flicking blood across Larson's foot. Of itself, Valvitnir jerked downward, severing the tendon behind Loki's knee.

Loki fell. Unable to use his right arm to catch himself, he dropped, face first, to the mud. Larson pressed Valvitnir's point to the back of his neck. The Trickster howled his frustration.

"Wait!" Loki's high-pitched voice betrayed fear.

Hatred, exhaustion, and grief warred within Larson, warping intellect in a gray haze of confusion. Despite its frightened quality, Loki's command held an inviolate authority. Larson paused.

Loki continued quickly. "If you kill me, you destroy your own world."

Loki's voice inspired violent hatred in Larson for this god who had twisted Silme's half brother into a vindictive demon and designed the ruin of gods and men. Abhorrence flared toward the god whose ugly daughter possessed Silme's soul. "Die, you scum!" He arched Valvitnir to gain momentum. The blade leaped hungrily for Loki's neck.

Loki loosed a cry, half sob and half scream. "Your mother's blood is on your hands!"

Inches from Loki, Larson pulled his blow. The accusation seared like a hot knife, but he dared not display weakness before the Trickster. "Explain," was all he trusted himself to say.

Vidarr's presence intervened, weaker than a whisper. *Caution, Allerum. He'll trap you, too.*

Larson pressed Valvitnir tighter to Loki's neck. Though the sword fought Larson's restraint, he forced it steady. A second mental being poked gently into Larson's mind, more powerful than the first and as beautiful as the god at his mercy. *If you slay me, no one will contest Odin. The Norse pantheon will endure, supreme through eternity. Christianity can never reign. Al Larson, if you kill me, your world, your family, and the people you loved will never exist!*

Never exist . . . never exist. . . . The last phrase reverberated through Larson's mind and no original thought replaced it. Loki's mental essence reached for a memory.

No! Vidarr blocked Loki like a physical entity. *You can't . . .*

Stop me! Loki's far stronger presence thrust Vidarr aside effortlessly. Larson remained motionless, his eyes fixed on Gaelinar, who struggled to his feet, still dazed by Loki's magics.

The sky seemed to open. Sunlight streamed through the clouds, accompanied by the moist heat of a New Hampshire summer. Hvergelmir's roar became the crackle of a campfire. The mingled reek of mold and death transformed to the lighter aroma of pine. Larson watched himself with the detachment of a movie. He was twelve years old.

"Al!" The familiar voice of his father rose over the rustle of grasses in the wind. "Let your sister tend the fire. You've got more important things to do. I promised you'd teach your brother to fly his kite."

Larson felt his heart quicken at the sound of his father's voice. He watched himself trot across a plain of weeds to where his father stood beside his little brother, Timmy. Spectator to his own memory, Larson examined his father with a stranger's eye. Carl Larson was a large man, powerful yet gentle. His close-cropped, blond hair had a tendency to stand on end, giving him an air of harshness. But his soft, blue eyes betrayed him.

The vivid vision of the dead father he loved

brought tears to Larson's eyes. Instantly, the scene changed. Larson saw his mother kneeling beside the dented fender of his father's brand new Plymouth. Tears blurred her pale eyes and drew crooked lines through the blush on her cheeks. It took Larson several seconds to recognize the child at her side, himself at age five, torn by his mother's sorrow.

He remembered the scene well. Planning to take the Plymouth for its first test drive, Cindy Larson had backed the car into the garage wall. "Tell him I did it," Al Larson told his frightened mother. The ridiculousness of his suggestion made her laugh through her tears. She hugged him to her chest, and Larson reveled in the memory of her warmth and the touch of her lips against his forehead.

"Mom!" Images dimmed, crumbled, and reformed in a different sequence. He heard his father's cheers, mixed with the goading cries of other parents. A soccer ball whuffed toward Larson's knee. Twisting sideways, he stopped the ball's momentum with his calf, dribbled several paces forward, and kicked a pass to the right wing. A crowd of players overran Larson's position at fullback. As the ball reversed direction, they turned and raced after it.

The shrill of a whistle called the first half to its conclusion. Larson took his turn at the water bottle and sat on the bench. His closest friend, soccer hero Tom Jeffers, dropped to the seat at his side. "Nice block, Larson."

Larson combed hair from his eyes with his fingers. "Thanks, T.J. You're doing pretty good yourself. Think we'll catch them in the second half?"

"Think?" Jeffers winked at a girl on the sidelines. "I know it, man. I'll put in a couple shots. You just keep them scoreless."

Larson watched the girl blush and turn away, slightly jealous of his friend's rugged good looks. "Talk to the goalie. I can't make a promise like that."

Jeffers met Larson's stare, and the center forward's face waxed pensive. "I got a promise for you. Keep them scoreless next half, and I'll get you a date for the prom with my sister."

"Terry?" Larson's voice rose in surprise and excitement. He cleared his throat and continued at his normal octave. "You serious?"

Jeffers laughed. "Yeah. Sure. Just play that defense. I want to win this one."

"Yeah. Sure." Larson's mind turned from the game to a picture of Terry Jeffers. Long-legged, dark-haired, blue-eyed, Terry Jeffers could find her own share of dates. And he never possessed the courage to ask her.

Jeffer's voice and his heavy hand clamped to Larson's shoulder pulled the fullback from his reverie. "So what are you doing after graduation?"

"I don't know. College, I think. What about you?"

Jeffer's started toward center field. "I'm joining the army. *Going to Vietnam to become a war hero . . .*"

Larson's memory broke with jarring abruptness. He felt his consciousness jolted to the path of a different recollection. It was the summer after his high school graduation. Seeking spending money for college, he found a job working as a day camp counselor. The pay was comparatively high for employment of its type, and the benefits undeniable. Camp Collinswood had two pools, four athletic fields, sixteen tennis courts, and fifty wooded

acres. Yet despite the many facilities, the boys in
Larson's group preferred a game which required
no special equipment.

Standing with his assistant before a dozen rowdy
seven- and eight-year-old boys, Larson heard himself ask. "What do you guys want to do now?"

"Kill the counselor!" they chanted, nearly in
unison. A wave of small bodies converged on Larson and his assistant. Resigned to the punches and
prods of children too young to inflict significant
pain, Larson alternated between feigned defense-
lessness and throws which sprawled the campers
in giggling heaps. He passed off wrestling moves
as karate throws, or tricks from his days of "alliga-
tor tussling" and "dinosaur hunting."

"Al's got a girlfriend. Al's got a girlfriend," one
of the youngsters chanted teasingly. Larson rose,
dumping two boys from his back. Terry Jeffers
stood several feet from the game. Her drab-colored
dress was rumpled, and her hands knotted together at her waist. As he drew closer, Larson
noticed her eyes, red and swollen, hollowed by
anguish.

"Terry. . . ?" he started uncertainly.

"Al." Her voice was a tenuous quaver. "It's . . ."

The scene shattered with Loki's muttered curse.
Larson's thoughts jumped to his prom with the
disquieting transition of a scratched record.

Terry wore a gown of blue satin. Dark hair
haloed her face in burnished waves. Eye shadow
and mascara focused attention on the sapphire
depths of her eyes. Breathless, Larson stared. But
his thoughts drifted back toward the unfinished
sentence of his previous memory. Somehow, Larson knew Terry's message was extremely important.

Loki's presence nudged Larson back toward his

vision of Terry Jeffers before the prom. Each line
in the petals of her corsage blossomed into vivid
focus. Satin swirled about her slender hips. . . .

Damn you, Trickster! Vidarr shoved Larson's memories askew as the gods circled the flawed and
tangled circuitry of his mind with the caution of
dancers on a bed of needles.

. . . Terry's dress went black as death; her head
buried in her hands.

Loki snarled. Larson felt sanity slide beneath a
wash of terror.

. . . He danced to a slow ballad. Terry's head
rested against his shoulder. His sweating palms left
marks in the fine, blue satin of her dress. . . .

. . . But the feeling was all wrong. The music
muted to the heavy toll of bells, chilling harmony
to the anguished sobs of Mrs. Jeffers. Terry stared
at a closed coffin. And Larson remembered. *T.J.
died in Vietnam!*

Rationality broke beyond control of the spar-
ring gods. Thoughts merged in a disharmonic
orchestra of memory. Lights flashed as one: the
cold yellow of porchlight, the glaring red-orange
of mortars, the multi-hued explosions of sorceries.
Larson felt alternately hot as fire and cold as death.
Grief and hatred, sorrow and vengeance, self-pity
and empathy swirled to a numbing, incomprehensible mix of emotion which tore screams from his
throat.

Larson froze, listening to the echoes of his own
pained cries. Gradually, sanity drew his crumbled
thoughts together like pieces of a puzzle. *It was all
a lie, a world of men who sought honesty in falsehoods
and war in the name of peace. They preached "turn the
other cheek" and practiced "kill or be killed." We believed in death for freedom, and honor, yet dismembered*

*the dead without respect. I've seen too much fear and not
enough glory, a single God who promised forgiveness
and banished his children to hellish tortures for their
doubts and uncertainties. My country trained its babies
to kill, then condemned them as murderers.*

"Larson!" Loki's plea jerked Larson back to the
present. Gaelinar stood watching, his eyes dark
with concern. Again, Larson raised Valvitnir, its
steel a dull, gray shadow in the mist. His arm rose
and fell. The blade sheared through Loki's back,
the god's death justified by the lives of the innocent, the unborn casualties of future wars. And
Larson wept for the other casualties, men and
women whose existence became nothing more sub-
stantial than his memories of them. His own existence became a paradox, a life from a future which
was no longer reality.

Vidarr's mental presence whispered softer than
wind. *I'm sorry.*

The words struck Larson like a physical blow.
He stared at the sword in his fist; fresh blood
trickled from its haft to stain his fingers scarlet. *It
was all another lie.* Despite the utter destruction
Larson wreaked upon his own world, Vidarr remained imprisoned in the sword.

"Damn your evil heart!" Larson jumped to his
feet and hurled Valvitnir. The sword flipped end
over end, glittering as it passed beneath tears in
the clouds. "Damn all gods and men! You forced
my hand against everyone I loved in both worlds."
Turning his back on the sword which had served
as his companion for weeks in a strange land,
Larson staggered several paces. He collapsed at
Silme's side. Her flesh was cold to his touch. Her
lids remained closed, as if in sleep. Tears poured

from Larson's eyes like a miniature replica of Hvergelmir's falls.

Larson watched Gaelinar move through a grief-inspired haze which gave all reality the consistency of dream. Respectfully, the Kensei averted his eyes from Larson's tears. He trotted forward and seized the blooded Helsword which still lay beside Bramin's soulless body.

"You stand for everything I despise and against everything I believe." Gaelinar's voice sounded strangely solid in the lingering silence which followed Larson's mental battle. Several seconds passed before Larson realized his teacher addressed the sword.

Larson heard no reply, but the sword shimmered in Gaelinar's hand and its form blurred. Numbly, he watched the Kensei carry the blade to Hvergelmir's chasm and set it, point first, at the edge of the falls.

Sound rose from the warped swordshape, scarcely loud enough to rise above the water's roar. "Back, mortal fool. You've no right to challenge gods."

The shifting mists before Gaelinar revealed a vague man form. Shock weakened Larson's grasp, and Silme's body slipped to the ground. Kensei Gaelinar cleared his throat. "God or man, Helblindi, you've no right to take glory from a warrior's battles. You're a tool of chaos and evil, a being with no reason to live."

Helblindi's figure sharpened to clarity. Though golden-haired and fair-skinned as Loki, Helblindi displayed none of his brother's beauty. "Men, not gods, are tools, mortal. Your weaknesses shall become my strengths. You're a toy, swordsman. I'll crush you with your own flaws."

The bitterness and power in the god's voice

made Larson flinch. But Gaelinar stood steady as the land itself. "I have no flaws. Ask Allerum." Gaelinar's foot lanced toward the god, faster than thought. The blow crashed into Helblindi's gut. Off-balanced, the god fell, twisting and screaming, into the cascade. Gaelinar completed his statement in a triumphant whisper. "I'm no hero."

Awe nearly deafened Larson to a noise from behind. Even as he whirled, he knew what he would find. The spell which had imprisoned Helblindi in a sword was the same which held Vidarr. As promised by the Fates, Loki's death did break his enchantments; they just took time to fade. Larson recognized Vidarr from mental images and the broken reality of Vietnam. Though freed, the god still addressed him telepathically, but now Vidarr's actual presence was undetectable in his mind. *I owe you, Allerum. Ask what you wish. If it is within my power, it is yours.*

Larson did not hesitate for consideration. "Silme . . ."

Vidarr's face looked stricken. *Allerum, I'm sorry. I want her back as much as you do. If you had used any other sword . . .*

What little strength remained to Larson dispersed. He turned away.

There is something I can do.

Larson heard nothing. He cradled Silme's body like a doll. Both his lost world and the one he had come to save seemed faded and distant as childhood dreams. Vidarr's presence materialized in his mind. The god enfolded his charge, flicking consciousness to peace, and Larson dropped into a twilight sleep.

While Larson lay, anesthetized by Vidarr's powers, the god set to his task. Larson's mind patterns stretched before him like a road map designed by a maniac. Vidarr sighed without bitterness. With the tenderness of a father with his child, he sliced blind loops and alleys. His will forced coiled paths straight, broke unrelated connections, reaffixed the frayed thought waves which allowed Bramin and Loki to torture Larson with memory.

Vidarr's work continued well into the afternoon. The god mended all the flaws his capabilities allowed, deleting only those ideas which Larson found intolerable. He left the recollections of Vietnam, T.J.'s funeral, and Larson's own death along with happier ones of his parents and Terry in her prom dress. Though painful, they belonged to Larson and had their role in shaping his personality. Vidarr had no wish to change his savior, only to restore the sanity which was his by right of birth.

As the last of the tortuous pathways assumed its proper place, Vidarr withdrew to assess his work with pride. He retreated from Larson's mind, leaving a final message of hope and peace, a promise of future happiness and pain in a world with elves, dwarves, gods, and magic. Then Vidarr disappeared for Asgard, mentally and physically, leaving Larson with little or no understanding of his reward. *Farewell, Allerum.*

EPILOGUE

*"Every man takes the limits of his own
field of vision for the limits of the world."*
—*Arthur Schopenhauer*,
Studies in Pessimism

Still dazed, Larson watched Gaelinar examine the long row of weapons spread before him on the dirt. A half dozen steel shurikens weathered the Kensei's gaze. Each sharpened corner underwent and passed the test of Gaelinar's thumbnail, and he dropped the shurikens in the grass. Next, the swordmaster turned his attention to a silver chain, tipped at both ends by a five-inch spike. Every link met Gaelinar's intense scrutiny before the Kensei set the manrikigusari aside with the same satisfaction.

Stung by Gaelinar's insensitive disregard for the three corpses and for his own sorrow, Larson abandoned Silme's body and moved toward the Kensei.

Gaelinar looked up briefly, smiled a greeting, and returned his attention to an instrument which resembled a large tuning fork with unequal blades. This, too, the Kensei set aside. He reached for a dagger, unsheathed it, frowned, and wiped a spot on the blade with his cloak. With a toss of his head, he set the edge of the steel to his whetstone and scraped.

Annoyance rose in Larson. He waited for his teacher to speak.

Gaelinar said nothing. He nodded approval at the knife, sheathed it, and placed it with his other weapons. Katana and shoto soon joined his arsenal, along with a small knife which slid from a position in the katana's sheath. Larson had not previously noticed it.

Gaelinar hefted a short metal band and flared it into a fan with recklessly sharp edges. Larson's discomfort exploded into anger. "You inhuman bastard!"

Gaelinar looked up.

Larson paced furiously. "How can you sit there prissing and preening while Silme lies there dead? You're wrong! You do have flaws. You're not a man, you're an insensitive beast, a stone without feelings. Silme is dead! Can't you understand that? Can't you even cry?" Grief crushed wrath, and Larson was overcome by a fresh bout of tears. "Damn you!"

Gaelinar made no reply. A deft flick of his wrist closed the fan. Slowly, he reached for his arsenal. He tied the manrikigusari around his waist, beneath the wide sash. The swords and dagger regained their places at his sides. He stuffed the hachiwari in his belt, behind the katana. The metal fan disappeared beneath his cloak. Carefully, Kensei Gaelinar set to work, arranging each shuriken in its proper position in its arm sheath.

Each moment of silence jabbed Larson like a knife. He cursed the Kensei in Old Norse, switched to English as he expended his repertoire of insults, then finished in the Vietnamese version of American.

Gaelinar seemed to take no notice. He finished his housekeeping efficiently, patted the hilt of his katana, and finally turned his attention to his raving companion. "You coming?"

Larson bit his lip, having exhausted his supply of oaths, blasphemies, and affronts. "Where?" was all he managed to say.

Gaelinar studied the foaming hybrid of waters which formed the falls of Hvergelmir. "To Hel. I'm bringing Silme back."

Larson's eyes widened. His nostrils flared. He found himself utterly incapable of speech.

Gaelinar continued. "In the chasm, beyond the Helspring, is a bridge which leads to Hel."

Larson found his tongue. "You're crazy! Vidarr said he couldn't . . ."

Gaelinar interrupted, his stare distant. "Vidarr's only a god. Together, we've already killed two, Helblindi without even a weapon. There's only one left." His gaze met Larson's, and the elf looked away. Gaelinar's tone went grim. "Allerum, you made a promise to Silme. You vowed that if this quest doomed the two of you to separate worlds, you would find her."

"But that was when I thought . . ." began Larson in defense.

Gaelinar waved him silent. "You think too much. I'm going after her. Are you coming?"

Larson chewed his lower lip and turned away. He heard the rustle of grasses as Gaelinar walked toward the narrow path into Hvergelmir's valley.

Gods. Larson approached Loki's body, examining the dark blood which had clotted around his fatal stroke *Even for the remote possibility of retrieving Silme's soul, I can't face another god.*

Can I?

The rush of cascading rivers and the howl of wind were his only answers. Gaelinar's golden figure marched on toward Hel's pathway. Gritting his teeth against what he might see, Larson rolled Loki's body to its back. The god's face seemed as handsome in death as in life. His oddly-colored eyes still glimmered. "Good-bye, noble foe," said Larson softly. He caught Loki's rigid arm and flipped the body into the Helspring.

Loki tumbled limply through the surge of intertwined rivers and was soon lost beneath the boiling current of white water. Larson caught up Loki's sword and scrambled after the Kensei.

Gaelinar stopped as Larson approached. He waited until the elf drew to his side. "Yeah," Larson said softly. "I'm coming." They turned toward the narrow pathway together.

For some distance, man and elf picked their way down the incline in silence. Larson paused a moment in thought, then confronted his companion. "Gaelinar?"

"Hmmm?"

"While we're at it, can we free Brendor, too?"

Kensei Gaelinar's smile was slight, but unmistakable. His arm pressed to Larson's shoulder. "Sure, hero. You can only die once."

DAW

Discover the Enchantment of
Michael Moorcock

Elric of Melniboné
ELRIC AT THE END OF TIME.
Come with the Prince of Melnibone as he ventures to the very
end of time itself, standing beside the immortals as Chaos
launches its last great assault on a crumbling universe.
(UE2228—$3.50)

The Runestaff Series
Dorian Hawkmoon fell under the power of the Runestaff, a
mysterious artifact more ancient than time itself. Its spell shaped
a destiny that involved Hawkmoon in strange, destructive
schemes and in wild, uncanny adventures in distant places as
he battled to the death the evil forces of the Dark Empire that
threatened to betray his very heritage. The Runestaff novels
are among the great classics of fantastic adventure.

☐ **THE JEWEL IN THE SKULL** (UE2175—$2.95)

☐ **THE MAD GOD'S AMULET** (UE2216—$2.95)

☐ **THE SWORD OF THE DAWN** (UE2173—$2.95)

☐ **THE RUNESTAFF** (UE2218—$2.95)

NEW AMERICAN LIBRARY
P.O. Box 999, Bergenfield, New Jersey 07621

Please send me the DAW BOOKS I have checked above. I am enclosing $_____
(check or money order—no currency or C.O.D.'s). Please include the list price plus
$1.00 per order to cover handling costs. Prices and numbers are subject to change
without notice.

Name _____

Address _____

City _____ State _____ Zip _____
Please allow 4-6 weeks for delivery.